*Joseph Connolly*

# The Book Quiz Book

*Penguin Books*

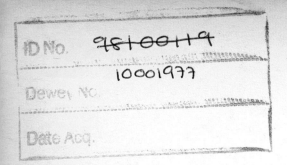

Penguin Books Ltd, Harmondsworth, Middlesex, England
Viking Penguin Inc., 40 West 23rd Street, New York, New York 10010, U.S.A.
Penguin Books Australia Limited, Ringwood, Victoria, Australia
Penguin Books Canada Limited, 2801 John Street, Markham, Ontario,
Canada L3R 1B4
Penguin Books (N.Z.) Ltd, 182–190 Wairau Road, Auckland 10, New Zealand

First published 1985

Copyright © Joseph Connolly, 1985
All rights reserved

Made and printed in Great Britain by
Cox & Wyman Ltd, Reading
Typeset in 9/11pt Linotron Century Schoolbook by
Rowland Phototypesetting Limited, Bury St Edmunds, Suffolk

*For Kingsley.*
*Chiss, mite.*

Contents

# Contents

# Foreword

Now I don't know whether you've ever undergone the faintly hilarious experience of trying to sell the idea for a book to any publishers, but if by now you are laughing fatly you will know that they are invariably courteous and encouraging right up to the point when they throw you out. The idea is usually annihilated by the money-man. Initially they think they might possibly be able to sell a few dozen copies to mindless derelicts who know no better, and that – bulked out by a library sale – might conceivably render the project viable, so long as the author presses for no more than a Greek and boozy lunch and his bus fare home. And only *then* do they hope sincerely that you can place it elsewhere, without delay.

But this was not at all the way when I accosted the head Penguin with the germ of this little gem. His old black wings clapped like the dickens, so excited was he – fifty years on and but at the threshold of his prime. 'Marvellous!' he cawed (yes, for the benefit of the sceptics and naturalists among you, Penguins caw). 'Stupendous! Colossal! Give me more!' And stuff like that. I glowed with authorial pride; who wouldn't?

'There's just one thing,' he added.

Suddenly, the formality of his tone was in accord with his attire. 'There's just one thing' is what the well-bred among us utter while the rest say 'but'. But however you cut it, the heart sinks – not so much like a stone, but more like those little plastic submarines one used to get free in Corn Flakes during the fifties, I don't know if you remember them; one was supposed to fill them with *baking powder*, of all bizarre concoctions, and when set in a bath they were meant to go up and down and up and down but what they actually did was go down and stay there and the baking powder turned the water to paste and what I am getting at is that that is how it is when a publisher enthuses and then says 'but' – or, in the case of Penguin Number One, 'there's just one thing'. I sucked my hack's quill and waited for more. 'What exactly', he intoned (yes, they can do that too) 'is your potential market? At whom are we pitching, precisely?'

I was thrown, and I confess it. I naïvely assumed that we were pitching at anyone gullible enough to part with the hard-earned in exchange for a collection of conundrums which would squander their time, pebbledash their brains, and ultimately leave them feeling wretchedly ill-informed. Surely a publisher could pick no holes in that? What I mean to say is, that is the *meaning* of marketing, surely. But apparently not. 'What *sort* of man or woman are we aiming at?' King Penguin persisted. 'What can the purchaser expect?'

Well, I was as fogged as any mere author at synopsis stage. I even toyed with blurting that which one must *never* do – viz. that I hadn't a *clue* what the purchaser could expect as I hadn't written the bloody thing yet and was myself hovering upon the brink of amazement and panic over whether the deadline could even be met at all and feeling far from projecting some sort of sculptural *form* that was destined for a particular audience, lovingly hewn from among the masses.

But – as I began to work the thing – so such a form did emerge, rather bafflingly, and now and only now (when it is too late for Lord Penguin to change his mind about printing the thing) am I ready to set down *exactly* what the reader may expect. (Actually, for 'reader' do go on reading 'purchaser'; God knows, we all have a living to earn, and I simply refuse to believe that there are people mean enough to browse through a paperback to the extent of having reached thus far into the Foreword.)

What the said punters may expect, then, is a series of diverse, enlightening, amusing literary quizzes and puzzles, the solutions to some of which will be known to them, while those to others will be a revelation. There will also be questions which will strike them as flippant, tricksy, too-clever-by-half or even plain gobbledygook, and at times they could be right. The answers are, in many cases, far lengthier than the questions posed, usually because they are riveting, and sometimes for the reason that if you had spent as long as I have on research, you would be damned if anyone thought you might throw it all away merely on a line or two. The questions, indeed – although great for showing off and boring people at the sort of get-togethers you doubtless attend – might even be seen to be but a device for arriving at the literary information at the end of the ramble, for the book *could* be seen to be a sort of literary ramble – a stroll taken for pleasure, with much of interest along the way. What you may confidently expect, then, is a measured perambulation during the course of which it should become evident that both the journey *and* the arrival matter.

I am acutely aware that all of the foregoing might be so much bilge and that in fact the book's just a load of puzzles cobbled together, but put *that* in a synopsis and the Penguin God would have flapped like a nun and turned the whole thing down flat – and where would we all be then, that's what I should like to know.

As it is, I didn't, he didn't, and here it is.

Joseph Connolly
Hampstead
July 1985

**Part One**

????????????????????????????????

**The Questions**

# Food and Drink

The above indulgences positively permeate the following questions, and – unlike the quick-fire stuff – I urge you to wallow in them for as long as it pleases you. Food and drink are both, after all, things that should never be bolted, as we have all probably discovered by now. One way and another.

1. During the course of his Preface to a new edition of one of his novels, who was of the opinion that it was 'infused with a kind of gluttony, for food and wine, for the splendours of the recent past, and for rhetorical and ornamental language, which now with a full stomach I find distasteful'?

    And which novel was he referring to?

2. Whose exhortation is this: 'Claret is the liquor for boys; port for men; but he who aspires to be a hero must drink brandy'?

    Easy? Well, then, which young man set up the following plaintive cry: 'O, for a draught of vintage!'?

3. 'She believed he had been drinking too much of Mr Weston's good wine.'

    Who believed such a thing of whom? And in what novel, written by whom?

    And who used the quotation for the title of a novel of his own?

4. Which of the following references to wine are attributable to the Bible (extra kudos for Chapter and Verse) and which to Shakespeare (ditto for knowing the play)? One of them, just to make it more interesting,

Answers on page 101

comes from neither. Can you spot it? And can you identify it?

a. 'Be not drunk with wine'
b. 'Eat thy bread with joy, and drink thy wine with a merry heart'
c. 'Good wine is a good familiar creature if it be well used'
d. 'A flask of wine, a book of verse – and thou beside me singing in the wilderness'
e. 'Like the best wine, for my beloved, that goeth down sweetly, causing the lips of those that are asleep to speak'
f. 'What life is then to a man that is without wine? For it was made to make men glad'
g. 'Wine loved I deeply'
h. 'Use a little wine for thy stomach's sake'
i. 'Wine is a mocker, strong drink is raging'

5. Who wrote the following?
   Despite the titles, of course, none of them has anything whatever to do with food or drink, as you know. Well – *one* of them has, actually. Any ideas?

a. *The Ginger Man*
b. *A Taste of Honey*
c. *Tristram Shandy*
d. *Wine in Peace and War*
e. *Cakes and Ale*
f. *Eggs, Beans and Crumpets*
g. *The Onion Eaters*
h. *An Ice-Cream War*
i. *Chicken Soup With Barley*

6. Who wrote this – as recently as 1984?
   I must add that Lawrence Durrell, who lives not far away, and whom I hadn't seen for a long while, reminded me that many years ago, about 1950, he and I happened to meet in Nîmes and that I com-

plained angrily about the local food, swearing that I would never go back to the region.

The clue (for I think it needs *some* sort of a clue) is that the subject under discussion here is not Lawrence Durrell, but the *food*.

**7.**
> Oh! The roast beef of England,
> And old England's roast beef.

The above, as everyone knows, was of course written by W. S. Gilbert. Or do I mean Noël Coward? Or do I mean neither?

**8.** A bubbly question. Who is talking about champagne? Where?

*a.* 'Champagne certainly gives one werry gentlemanly ideas, but for continuance, I don't know but I should prefer mild hale.'

*b.*
> The accursed power which stands on Privilege
> (And with Women, and Champagne, and
>     Bridge)
> Broke – and Democracy resumed her reign,
> (Which goes well with Bridge, and Women and
>     Champagne).

*c.* 'The Taittinger '45?'
'A fine wine, monsieur,' said the sommelier. 'But if monsieur will permit,' he pointed with his pencil, 'the Blanc de Blanc 1943 of the same mark is without equal.'

*d.* I had my secret and sure defence, like a talisman worn in the bosom, felt for in the moment of danger, found and firmly grasped. So I told him what in fact was not the truth, that I usually had a glass of champagne about that time, and asked him to join me.

*e.* 'There is no one so radical as a manservant whose freedom of the champagne bin has been interfered with.'

And finally – in order to prick the bubble, if not to swizzle the wine – where do we hear quite a bit about Sillery?

9. Well, who *did* actually say, 'Let them eat cake'? And why on earth was it said?

10. The speaker in the second quotation would appear to be going along at least wholeheartedly with the dictat of the proclaimer in the first. Two very different people talking, though – and each as famous. Who the blazes?

   a.  'Medical research has established, sir, that the ideal diet is one in which the animal and vegetable foods are balanced. A strict vegetarian diet is not recommended by the majority of doctors, as it lacks sufficient protein and in particular does not contain the protein which is built up of the amino acids required by the body. Competent observers have traced some cases of mental disorder to this shortage.'

   b.  'The trouble is,' he explained to Vesper, 'not how to get enough caviar, but how to get enough toast with it. Now,' he turned back to the menu. 'I myself will accompany mademoiselle with the caviar, but then I would like a very small tournedos, underdone, with "sauce Bearnaise" and a "coeur d'artichaut". While mademoiselle is enjoying the strawberries, I will have half an avocado pear with a little French dressing. Do you approve?'

## Quick-Fire Quiz

You will find quite a few of these twenty-question quick-fires scattered around the book. The idea is to take not *too* long pondering over each question – and, if the quiz is being done orally, to keep the questions coming fairly rapidly. That way, you can infuriate the person you are hurling them at, while glorying in a fatly complacent way at all those hissed 'oh, of *course!*' type remarks, when you rather decently supply the answer.

Fifteen correct out of twenty is seen to be competent-plus, while twenty out of twenty is visibly insufferable.

### Nineteenth-Century Works

All of the following are nineteenth-century works. All I require is their authors, as I expect that dates as well would be too much to hope for.

1. *The Coral Island*
2. *Treasure Island*
3. *Around the World in Eighty Days*
4. *The Antiquary*
5. *The History of Henry Esmond*
6. *Born in Exile*
7. *American Notes*
8. *The Eustace Diamonds*
9. *Many Cargoes*
10. *The Aspern Papers*
11. *Germinal*
12. *Silas Marner*
13. *Hereward the Wake*
14. *Wee Willie Winkie*
15. *Widowers' Houses*
16. *The Master of Ballantrae*
17. *The Duchess of Padua*

*Answers on page 105*

18. *Sylvia's Lovers*
19. *The House of the Seven Gables*
20. *The Well-Beloved*

---

## Quotation Titles

The titles of the following books are all quotations from earlier works. Author of each, please, and — more to the point – the sources of the quotations.

1. *Far from the Madding Crowd*
2. *The Mirror Crack'd from Side to Side*
3. *Gaudy Night*
4. *My Sad Captains*
5. *Cakes and Ale*
6. *For Whom the Bell Tolls*
7. *Blithe Spirit*
8. *The Darling Buds of May*
9. *The Doors of Perception*
10. *Cover Her Face*
11. *Dusty Answer*
12. *Love and Fame*
13. *Golden Apples of the Sun*
14. *The Ides of March*
15. *Of Mice and Men*
16. *Old Mortality*
17. *Brave New World*
18. *All Passion Spent*
19. *The Power and the Glory*
20. *Tender is the Night*

*Answers on page 106*

## The Things Men (and Women) Do

You have to know more than titles and authors for this one – it is the quiz that sorts out the readers from the bluffers. Below we have twenty leading characters from twenty important and well-known works – but from each and every period. Who are these people? And where do they come from?

1. A mean businessman who is visited by his partner on Christmas Eve.
2. A lad apprenticed to an undertaker, who escapes reality via his fantasies.
3. A military captain who is billeted to a country house he knows well from before the war.
4. A lady who is wooed by a shepherd, a farmer and a soldier, and marries two of them.
5. An orphan girl, sent to an institution, who later falls in love with a man with a mad wife.
6. A young man who works at the Town Hall, and marries the boss's daughter in order to further himself, despite being in love with an older woman.
7. A seventeen-year-old, bent upon becoming a gangster, who marries a sixteen-year-old in order to prevent her testifying against him in court.
8. A linen-weaver who is driven away by his neighbours by a false accusation of theft, and takes solace in his gold.
9. A Nottingham factory-worker who works furiously all week at a job he hates, in order to drink the proceeds at the weekend.
10. A jazz-loving graduate from a 'white-tile' university married to a colonel's daughter, and infuriated by his status.

*Answers on page 109*

11. A man who loved 'everything that's old', and whose house is mistaken for an inn by his guests, and his daughter mistaken for a servant.
12. An obsessive clerk who spends his football pool winnings upon kidnapping a girl.
13. A Muslim doctor in India, whose esteem for the British is turned to bitterness as a result of his having been shamed.
14. A boy (his mother is an innkeeper) who goes to sea with a squire and outwits pirates.
15. An eleven-year-old, born in Shanghai, separated from his parents in the confusion of Pearl Harbor, and interned in a Japanese camp for four years.
16. A small fellow who loved his underground home, and whose peace was disturbed by the arrival of 'dwarves'.
17. A man who decides upon assignations with two married women because they each hold the key to their husbands' wealth, and who ends up pinched by mock fairies.
18. A man failed in his attempt to dominate the world, who kills the wife of the spy responsible, only hours after the two were married.
19. A boy who had no mother, who teaches three children how to fly.
20. Someone inveigled by his aunt to become involved in the theft of an eighteenth-century cow creamer in order to retain for the services of the household the greatest chef in the world while pouring oil on the troubled waters of a lover's tiff and also trying to coax an uncle's blessing so that the said uncle's niece might marry a curate – all of which might have gone better but for the absence of a blessed policeman's helmet.

# Quick-Fire Quiz

### Who Wrote (Twentieth Century)?

Now this is a perfectly straightforward *Who Wrote?* quiz, with the added clue, if clue it be, that not only are all of the following twentieth-century works, but each of them is the *first* commercially published work of the author concerned – and they are all big-name authors, I promise you. More or less.

1. *Pied Piper of Lovers*
2. *The Brightfount Diaries*
3. *The Pothunters*
4. *Bright November*
5. *The Mystic Masseur*
6. *The Sweets of Pimlico*
7. *A Weekend with Claude*
8. *Babbling April*
9. *Whoroscope*
10. *A Standard of Behaviour*
11. *Dangling Man*
12. *The Sweet-Shop Owner*
13. *Mount Zion*
14. *Lord Malquist and Mr Moon*
15. *Eating People is Wrong*
16. *Tribute to Wordsworth*
17. *Time for a Tiger*
18. *Grimus*
19. *A Summer Bird-Cage*
20. *Captain Slaughterboard Drops Anchor*

*Answers on page 110*

## Children's Books

Although children's books crop up in a lot of the quizzes in this book, I thought that a number of classics deserved a space of their own. The following questions will be most enjoyed by confirmed nostalgics and parents – *actual* children won't stand much of a hope, I shouldn't have thought; although *your* children might well prove the exception.

1. Do you have an inkling as to who 'The Inklings' might be? With as much detail as possible, please.

2. In which series of books did Mr Wilkins quite often go 'I – I – Cor – Wumph!'?

3. Roald Dahl is a phenomenon. Although his first book was for children (*The Gremlins*, 1943) it was not until 1961 that he saw fit to repeat the experiment, although three volumes of adult – and chillingly brilliant – short stories and a novel intervened. As well as being approved of by parents (parents usually approve only of the safe and the dull), he has also managed to become the firm favourite of the children themselves.

   And now the questions:

   a. Who went up in the Great Glass Elevator?
   b. Who encountered a Giant Peach?
   c. Who was Champion of the World?
   d. Who had Marvellous Medicine?
   e. Who was Fantastic?
   f. Who owned the Chocolate Factory?

   And, by way of a finale: Roald Dahl wrote the screenplay for the 1968 film *Chitty-Chitty-*

*Answers on page 111*

*Bang-Bang.* Who wrote the books upon which the film was based?

4. Aren't all the Beatrix Potter *Peter Rabbit* books Lovely? I mean, apart from the horrid ones, and the violent ones, and the rather cruel ones, and the ones that go on a bit? Aside from a few posthumously published oddities, there are an accepted twenty-three titles in the canon, and as the full awfulness of this question begins to dawn, let me spring it all in a rush: *name them!*

5. A quick *Who Wrote?* All very well-known children's stories, and all pretty big-time authors. Sorting them out can sometimes be a problem, though.

   a. *Little Women*
   b. *Little Lord Fauntleroy*
   c. *The Little Train*
   d. *The Story of Little Black Sambo*
   e. *The Little Prince*
   f. *Little Red Riding-Hood*
   g. *The Little White Bird*
   h. *Little Grey Rabbit*
   i. *Little Men*
   j. *The Little Mermaid*

6. Which children's books open with the following words?

   a.   The Mole had been working very hard all the morning, spring cleaning his little home.

   b.   In summer all right-minded boys built huts in the furze-hill behind the College – little lairs whittled out of the heart of prickly bushes, full of stumps, odd root-ends and spikes, but, since they were strictly forbidden, palaces of delight.

   c.   Once there were four children whose names were Peter, Susan, Edmund and Lucy. This story is about something that happened to them when they were sent away from London during the war because of the air-raids.

d.    Here is Edward Bear, coming downstairs now, bump, bump, bump, on the back of his head . . .

e.    Not all that long ago, when children were even smaller and people had especially hairy knees, there lived an old man of Lochnagar.

f.    It was seven o'clock of a very warm evening in the Seeonee hills when Father Wolf woke up from his day's rest, scratched himself, yawned, and spread out his paws one after the other to get rid of the sleepy feeling in their tips.

g.    It all began with William's aunt, who was in a good temper that morning, and gave him a shilling for posting a letter for her and carrying her parcels from the grocer's.

h.

   *My Sister Jane*
   And I say nothing – no, not a word
   About our Jane. Haven't you heard?
   She's a bird, a bird, a bird, a bird.
   Oh it never would do to let folks know
   My sister's nothing but a great big crow.

i.    Once upon a time there was a little chimney-sweep, and his name was Tom. That is a short name, and you will have heard it before, so you will not have much trouble in remembering it.

j.    When Mary Lennox was sent to Missel-thwaite Manor to live with her uncle, everybody said she was the most disagreeable-looking child ever seen.

7. Lewis Carroll, as more or less everyone knows, was a pseudonym for the author of possibly the most famous children's book of all, and these questions are devoted to him.

a. What was his real name?

    *b.* What are the subtitles of *Through the Looking-Glass* and *The Hunting of the Snark*?

    *c.* One would expect the first edition of *Alice's Adventures in Wonderland* to be both rare and expensive, but why do you think it is *desperately* rare, and quite *colossally* EXPENSIVE?

    *d.* In 1941, *The Hunting of the Snark* was reissued, with illustrations by what other great fantasist?

    *e.* Some *Alice* questions:

        *i.* Who begged Alice that she accept her own 'elegant thimble' as a prize?

       *ii.* Who enjoined Alice to 'have some wine' in an 'encouraging tone'?

      *iii.* Who was of the opinion that 'everything's got a moral, if only you can find it'?

      *iv.* Who cried, 'Curiouser and curiouser!'?

       *v.* Who instructed whom to 'begin at the beginning . . . and go on till you come to the end: then stop'?

**8.** *Beano* books, *Dandy* books and *Noddy* books are adored by children and, quite predictably, often vilified by parents. This is quite unfair. Without them, we could never have savoured the incomparable wonders of Dennis the Menace, Desperate Dan, Minnie the Minx, Roger the Dodger, the *superb* Bash Street Kids – and, of course, huffy old Big Ears and spoilsport Mr Plod (to say nothing of Noddy himself with his god-awful jangling bell and his little car forever making that infernal Parp-Parp noise).

    And now (at last) to the question: just how long, do you think, have these apparently timeless publications been with us? When was the first issue of the *Beano*, the first issue of the *Dandy*, and the first *Noddy* book?

# Quick-Fire Quiz

### Fictitious Characters

Below are some very well-known, and some lesser-known characters from famous books over the ages. We just have to know *which* books – and, of course, who wrote them. I shan't expect dates, but I shan't refuse them either.

1. Dicky Sludge
2. Jimmy Porter
3. Pinkie
4. John Jarndyce
5. Joe Lampton
6. Heathcliff
7. Ratty
8. Aloysius
9. Daisy Mutlar
10. Rosie
11. J.
12. Sergeant Troy
13. Old Gobbo
14. Aziz
15. Misha Fox
16. Leopold Bloom
17. Man Friday
18. Johnny Town-Mouse
19. Jake Richardson
20. Vladimir

*Answers on page 115*

# Quick-Fire Quiz

### Sleuth

No, I am not going to ask you who created Sherlock Holmes, or Maigret, or Hercule Poirot. But I should love to hear who wrote of the following detectives:

1. Max Carrados
2. Dr Thorndyke
3. Father Brown
4. J. G. Reeder
5. Albert Campion
6. Roderick Alleyn
7. Dr Gideon Fell
8. Philo Vance
9. Nero Wolfe
10. Van der Valk
11. Gideon of the Yard
12. John Appleby
13. Nigel Strangeways
14. Sergeant Cuff
15. Malcolm Sage
16. Inspector Joseph French
17. Inspector Ghote
18. Inspector Hanaud
19. Inspector Parker
20. Inspector Baynes

*Answers on page 116*

# Crossword

ACROSS

1. Pawnbroker cat lived in a cabin? (3)
3. What Nollekens made of Sterne (4)
5. Sweeney, for one (6)
9. Of an ancient region, destroyed in a chart (8)
10. In which Humpty might have sat (3,3)
11. She had a fear of flying, at first (5)
12. A novel by Mrs Henry II, for instance? (4,5)
15. MS could be in it (11)
19. *The Way of the World* is such a drama! (11)
22. Were penny dreadfuls renowned for this? (9)
24. Why didn't they ask Mary Ann? (5)
25. The last of the Mohicans, for example (6)
26. Those in the literary limelight may be made so beastly! (8)
27. Hugh – Joyce's critic (6)
28. Who is preceded by this, in the work of reference? (4)
29. Common thanks for Italian poet – so coming off (3)

DOWN

1. It is periodically chatty (6)
2. Golding's crab? (6)
3. He wrote 'devilled corned meat' – but no tea, we hear (9)
4. Backward drab (11)
6. Clare (Hardy) (5)
7. Piggy theory of attribution? (8)
8. If he were alive, Jack would – but we write it of the dead (3)
13. Authoress I've met – his little saint is smashed (6,5)

*Solution on page 117*

14. The garden. Steinbeck was east of it (4)
16. By Thackeray – writer menace! (9)
17. Farrar's boy, followed by alternative degrees (4)
18. 'N' has need to destroy Maugham's work! (8)
20. Graduate ruined rest at Trollope's place (6)
21. In company, these are said to be behind-hand (6)
23. It is said that this author is the top! (5)
25. Writer's agent (3)

## Scored Lead-On Quiz

Now listen carefully. Each of the ten numbered questions has two connected parts. Part *a* is (fairly) easy, and part *b* is (fairly) tough. If you can answer *only* part *a* you score one point, and move on to the next whole question, and try your luck there. If you can answer part *b* correctly, you score *two* points. If you are a real clever-Dick and can answer both parts *a* and *b*, you receive the maximum available for each whole question: three points. Thus it will be perceived that the top total available for this quiz is thirty points. Assessments of your score follow the answers – but I do urge the sport in you to give the questions at least a passing glance *first*.

1. *a.* By what title is *Memoirs of a Woman of Pleasure* better known?
   *b.* Who wrote it?

2. *a.* Who wrote *The Theory and Practice of Gamesmanship, or, The Art of Winning Games without Actually Cheating*?
   *b.* Name the three sequels (in order) that make up the quartet.

3. *a.* Who wrote *Gone with the Wind*?
   *b.* Name any one other work by the author.

4. *a.* Who wrote *The Tragical History of Dr Faustus*?
   *b.* Who wrote *The Tour of Dr Syntax in Search of the Picturesque*?

*Answers on page 118*

5. *a.* The last chapter of which nineteenth-century novel opens thus: 'Reader, I married him'?

   *b.* The last chapter of which nineteenth-century novel opens thus: 'Who can be in doubt of what followed'?

6. *a.* In *Nicholas Nickleby*, what is the name of the headmaster of Dotheboys Hall? First name, too.

   *b.* In Frank Richards's 'Greyfriars' books, what is the name of the form-master to Bunter and the Remove? First name, too.

7. *a.* Whose private detective character is Philip Marlowe?

   *b.* Whose private detective character is Sam Spade?

8. *a.* Who won the Booker Prize in 1984? With what book?

   *b.* Who won the Booker Prize in 1983? With what book?

9. *a.* Who wrote of J. Alfred Prufrock?

   *b.* Who wrote of Hugh Selwyn Mauberley?

10. *a.* *Three Men in a Boat, to Say Nothing of the Dog.* Author, please – and the names of the three men.

    *b.* The name of the dog?

## Famous Last Words

Well, the last words of these novels may or may not be famous in themselves, but the books (all English), I do assure you, are all quite ridiculously famous, and you have read the lot. *Are* endings memorable? It is to be hoped so.

1.  With the relation of this extraordinary circumstance, my reappearance in these pages comes to an end. Let nobody laugh at the unique anecdote here related. You are welcome to be as merry as you please over everything else I have written. But when I write of *Robinson Crusoe*, by the Lord it's serious – and I request you take it accordingly! When this is said, all is said. Ladies and gentlemen, I make my bow, and shut up the story.

2.  I gave her bowed head one last stare, then I was walking. Firmer than Orpheus, as firm as Alison herself, that other day of parting, not once looking back. The autumn grass, the autumn sky. People. A blackbird, poor fool, singing out of season from the willows by the lake. A flight of grey pigeons over the houses. Fragments of freedom, an anagram made flesh. And somewhere the stinging smell of burning leaves.

    *cras amet qui numquam amavit*
    *quique amavit cras amet*

3.  And here I was, with my knobkerrie in my hand, staring across at the enemy I'd never seen. Somewhere out of sight beyond the splintered tree-tops of Hidden Wood a bird had begun to sing. Without knowing why, I remembered that it was Easter Sunday. Standing in that dismal ditch, I could find no consolation in the thought that Christ was risen. I splashed back to the dug-out to call the others up for 'stand-to'.

*Answers on page 120*

4.  O Agnes, O my soul, so may thy face be by me when I close my life indeed; so may I, when realities are melting from me, like the shadows which I now dismiss, still find thee near me, pointing upward!

5.  I lingered round them, under that benign sky; watched the moths fluttering among the heath and hare-bells; listened to the soft wind breathing through the grass; and wondered how anyone could ever imagine unquiet slumbers, for the sleepers in that quiet earth.

6.  'L—d!' said my mother, what is all this story about? –
    A COCK and a BULL, said Yorick – And one of the best of its kind, I ever heard.

7.  Twelve voices were shouting in anger, and they were all alike. No question, now, what had happened to the faces of the pigs. The creatures outside looked from pig to man, and from man to pig, and from pig to man again, but already it was impossible to say which was which.

8.  'Well – poor little thing, 'tis to be believed she's found forgiveness somewhere! She said she had found peace!'
    'She may swear that on her knees to the holy cross upon her necklace till she's hoarse, but it won't be true!' said Arabella. 'She's never found peace since she left his arms, and never will again till she's as he is now!'

9.  The Welches withdrew and began getting into their car. Moaning, Dixon allowed Christine to lead him away up the street. The whinnying and clanging of Welch's self-starter began behind them, growing fainter and fainter as they walked on until it was altogether overlaid by the other noises of the town and by their own voices.

10. . . . or shall I wear a red yes and how he kissed me under the Moorish wall and I thought well as well him as another and then I asked him with my eyes

to ask again yes and then he asked me would I yes to say yes my mountain flower and first I put my arms around him yes and drew him down to me so he could feel my breasts all perfume yes and his heart was going like mad and yes I said yes I will Yes.

## Acrostic

The following questions take the form of cryptic crossword clues. When they are written into the grid, vertically the first letters of each answer will spell the name of an author, followed by the title of one of his or her works.

1. Eliot's 'the ides'? (11)
2. Herbert, initially (3)
3. Uncontrolled state of Roderick (6)
4. Pitch, it is said, Lewis's novel (4)
5. He ghosts writer? (5)
6. Back le bon prize (5)
7. 'Mr W.H.' (5)
8. Sex for household rascal (4)
9. Playwright, since double-O went mad (7)
10. She wrote her novel on Coward's paper (6,5)
11. Marryat's not difficult – rank? (10)
12. Marie-Louise de la Ramée (5)
13. Jane's abbey (10)
14. Queen of crime (6)
15. The time of Woolf's novel (5)

# Quick-Fire Quiz

## Semi-Titles

Just supply the missing words in these titles – while knowing the authors, of course.

1. *The Last Chronicle of . . .*
2. *Granite and . . .*
3. *Why Didn't They Ask . . .*
4. *The Tenant of . . .*

*Answers on page 122*

5. *Love among the . . .*
6. *The Beautiful and . . .*
7. *The Nigger of . . .*
8. *The Ordeal of . . .*
9. *Snooty . . .*
10. *Tinker, Tailor, Soldier . . .*
11. *The Heart of . . .*
12. *The Love-Girl and the . . .*
13. *Memento . . .*
14. *Girl . . .*
15. *After Many a . . .*
16. *The Posthumous Papers of . . .*
17. *The Desire and Pursuit of . . .*
18. *Shooting an . . .*
19. *The Portrait of . . .*
20. *The Picture of . . .*

# Call My Bluff

As with the irresistible TV programme, so with this – with one *slight* additional nuisance. There follow each strangeness *four* definitions, and not the usual three. I defend this by averring that it is easier when the possibilities are printed before you, rather than having to remember what the hell that damn man said, when you had been busy ogling Joanna Lumley or Arthur Marshall. Anyway, here are the words – *one* of the definitions is true, the rest gobbledegook.

1. ARMENIAN BOLE
   a. A form of polo, whereby wooden balls are struck with poles, as opposed to mallets, by a five-a-side mounted team. The game is

*Answers on page 122*

passingly referred to in Cervantes' *Don Quixote*, while a sophisticated version of it is described in Graham Greene's *Travels with My Aunt*.

b. A kind of red powdered chalk, available from a chemist – and not necessarily in Armenia – which, when mixed with water, becomes a paste that is employed by bookbinders prior to gilding. Sometimes, black lead is added to the mixture.

c. An expression invented by Kipling, and used by him exclusively in his *Stalky* books. It comes into the category of public school slang, and attempts to describe, in a derogatory manner, circumloquacious, flowery, exaggerated and wordy talk.

d. A thick rag paper, with an inordinately high fibre content and a waxy, three-dimensional grain. Much favoured in Japan for Zen brush painting, the twist of the grain becoming an active constituent of the work of art. Why it is referred to as 'Armenian' is a mystery.

2. CADWALLADER
   a. The name given to ostrich skin when it has been bleached and tanned for use by bookbinders. Because of the difficulty of obtaining large expanses of unblemished 'hide', it tends to be used only for detailed work, and is much favoured by modern binders as an inset lozenge.

   b. A bounder, a scoundrel – now, of course, popularly cad. The abbreviation occurred in the eighteenth century, we think, though an example of its original usage appears in Congreve's *The Way of the World*: 'I beg they'll admit *me* as one of their Privy Council, over this other fellow. No sort of a gentleman, sir – a cadwallader and a thoroughgoing jackanapes!'

c. Simply a surname. He comes up fairly briefly in Tobias Smollett's *Peregrine Pickle*, while a *Mrs* Cadwallader is mentioned in George Eliot's *Middlemarch*.

d. Not quite a pith helmet, but the Indian version of a Panama hat with a higher crown and a heavier brim. One is habitually carried by Aziz in E. M. Forster's *A Passage to India*, though less to wear than to fan himself, it seemed.

3. HERALD FROY

a. The mysterious and alluring character in Iris Murdoch's *Flight from the Enchanter*, who drove a 'very dark green Riley'. Murdoch has stated in an interview that of all her characters she hoped and thought that Froy might rank alongside some of those in Dickens as a strong and enduring fictional presence.

b. One of the members of the College of Arms, as chronicled by Sir Winston Churchill in his *History of the English-Speaking Peoples*. Founded in 1483, it comprised in addition to Herald Froy: Garter Principal King-of-Arms, Clarenceux King-of-Arms South of the Trent, Norroy King-of-Arms North of the Trent, Pursuivants Rouge Croix, Bluemantle, Rouge Dragon and Portcullis.

c. One of Keith Waterhouse's pseudonyms (another was Lee Gibb). Under the Froy name he published a couple of humorous books on the subject of marriage in 1957 and 1958. In 1959 his name was made with

*Billy Liar* – *not* published under a pseudonym.

d. The conscientious police officer assigned to the Dutch detective Van der Valk in the first of Nicholas Freeling's books, and who recurs throughout the series – usually as placator, pouring oil over troubled waters whenever Van der Valk clashes with his superiors.

4. GYPSY BREYNTON
   a. A book of girls' stories (1866) and one of the earliest writings of American novelist Elizabeth Stuart Phelps Ward (1844–1911). Her best-known work is *The Gates Ajar* (1868).

   b. A pseudonym employed by W. H. Davies for a series of several hundreds of poems published throughout the 1930s in the *Countryman*. They were collected into one volume by Jonathan Cape in 1941 – under Davies's own name, after his identity had been rumbled by Bernard Shaw.

   c. A tiny hamlet in Hampshire, whose chief claim to fame lies in its proximity to Selborne. It was here that the two distinguished naturalists Thomas Pennant and Daines Barrington put up, while advising Gilbert White on his *Natural History and Antiquities of Selborne* (1789).

   d. A character encountered by George Borrow in the course of his wanderings in *The Romany Rye* of 1857 – although he is first mentioned briefly in *Lavengro* (1851) in the company of Jasper Petulengro.

**5.** THE NUREMBERG CHRONICLE

    *a.* A series of 178 folio volumes, now held by a rabbinical body in Jerusalem, recording the proceedings of the post-war trials of those accused of Nazi war crimes. The printing takes the form of a parallel text (German/Hebrew) and a German/English version is housed in the British Library.

    *b.* A novel by Eric Ambler, published in 1939, following on from the success of *The Mask of Dimitrios*. He also wrote the screenplay for the film which was made in 1945, and re-entitled *Journey into Fear*.

    *c.* A monumental fifteenth-century German book depicting mainly scriptural subjects, and notable chiefly for the fact that it contains over two thousand woodcuts and printed illustrations provided by a team of artists – one of whom was the young Albrecht Dürer.

    *d.* A very short-lived non-political newspaper set up in 1954 by a group of like-minded authors and artists, one of whom was Heinrich Böll – his involvement partly a reaction to the critical hostility that greeted his novel *And Never Said a Word*. The paper appeared weekly for seven weeks, and then ran out of money, the projected aim for it to become an independent daily never realized.

**6.** MEMBRANAE

    *a.* Vellum notebooks used in ancient Rome, sometimes as an *aide-mémoire* for students, but more usually containing handwritten literature, and sold in the market-place. They are later than papyrus, precede the codex, and are mentioned once by Juvenal.

THE BOOK QUIZ BOOK 43

b. In the second part of Jonathan Swift's *Gulliver's Travels* (1726), when Gulliver is
cast ashore on Brobdingnad, where everyone is as tall as steeples, the king quizzes
him as to the ways of other lands, and
momentarily puzzles him by referring to
the Lilliputians (from Lilliput, the land of
tiny people) as Membranae.

c. A slim volume by Ezra Pound, published
initially in an edition of only five copies in
Milan in 1955, and then in a trade edition
by Pesce d'Oro (Milan) followed by an
American edition (New Directions) in
1956. The separate text was never published in Britain, but the work has now
been incorporated into Faber's *Collected
Shorter Poems*.

d. It is unclear as to quite *what* 'membranae'
are, but according to Walpole in Shaw's
*The Doctor's Dilemma* the formula for a
healthy constitution was as follows: 'the
removal by surgery of the membranae and
the nuciform sac, together with the
stimulation of the phagocytes'. And he
founded his reputation (and his fortune)
upon its practice.

7. OROSIUS

a. In the sixteenth century, a group of twenty
book covers were made in solid gold for
Duke Albrecht of Brandenburg. Although
of gold, with a silver-gilt filigree overlay,
the patterns follow those of leather bindings (bevelled edges and all) but each bears
a circular boss or medallion at its centre.
The name of this boss is an 'orosius' and
these twenty covers bear the most ornate
and best-known examples.

  *b.* A fifth-century Spanish monk, and author of *Historia adversus paganos*, which was not translated into English until the ninth century. He was a disciple of St Augustine, and his friendship with St Jerome is recorded.

  *c.* Orosius and Crispus are two of the Nazarenes in Anthony Burgess's *The Kingdom of the Wicked* (1985). Paul (or Saul of Tarsus) repeatedly advocates brotherly love and tolerance, though this pair seem never happier than when fighting or bloodletting.

  *d.* In the 1960s, Michael Foot was much concerned with the Socialist weekly *Tribune*, and contributed a long-running series of essays. For reasons best known to himself, he wished his authorship of these articles to be concealed, and, rejecting his previous literary pseudonym 'Cassius' as by now too well known, he this time selected 'Orosius'.

**8.** TRAPBOIS
  *a.* *Martha* Trapbois is an ascetic and austere character in Scott's *The Fortunes of Nigel*, while her father (referred to simply as 'Trapbois') is a miser, and only one of a galaxy of interesting minor characters, alongside Dame Ursula Suddlechop and Sir Hugo Malagrowther.

  *b.* In 1783, an enterprising Parisian bookseller named Jules Trapbois took a stroll along the banks of the Seine and saw many more people doing likewise than ever came past his shop. With no licence, he began selling books on Sunday afternoons on the Left Bank, and other booksellers and print-makers quickly followed; today, the familiar lock-up closets on the walls are still called after the man who subsequently designed the first of them: Trapbois.

c. George Savage Trapbois was one of Thackeray's several pseudonyms – his own favourite being Michael Angelo Titmarsh. Under the Trapbois name he published *The Great Hoggarty Diamond* (1841) and *The Fitzboodle Papers* (1844).

d. A 'trapbois' is a device first recorded in fifteenth-century Germany, though more widely employed in France and England, whereby a woodcutter's block is held firm upon an angled board while work is being done. Most extant examples are themselves of fruitwood with sprung metal clamps, and there is always a channel at its base to collect the parings.

9. THE GULS HORNEBOOKE
   a. A book of household management and cookery by Anna-Maria Gilpin, published in Edinburgh in 1851. All the recipes and homilies are of Scottish origin, however, and although the book was known and reasonably successful the advent of Mrs Beeton ten years later totally eclipsed the work.

   b. A satirical volume by Thomas Dekker, published in 1609. It takes the form of a sort of etiquette manual for fops and dandies – a parody of the 'courtesy' books of the period, and a potent attack upon that section of society detested by Dekker.

c. *The Guls Hornebooke* is a wholly fictitious work alluded to once only at the outset of Conan Doyle's story *Silver Blaze* by Dr Watson. He and Holmes had come freshly from seeing the book safely into the hands of its rightful owner, the Crown Prince of Bavaria, its retrieval having narrowly averted civil war in that country.

d. The sample-book of Theo Van Guls, master printer of Amsterdam, 1671–1753. It is a folio, and comprises forty-six alphabets – each of a differing typeface – the Lord's Prayer – again in differing faces and several languages – as well as thousands of printer's rules and devices – cartouches, fleurons, colophons and the like.

**10.** GUPPY

a. A children's book of 1934, subtitled *The Tale of a Mongrel Dog Nobody Wanted* and written by Eleanor Frances Lattimore, an American author better known for her many stories set in China, the first of which was called *Little Pear* (1931), which is the story of a five-year-old boy.

b. A guppy is a scalpel-like instrument used by bookbinders for blind-stamping, embossing and impressing gold leaf into cover and spine decoration. Its 'blade' may be as fine as a needle, or up to a quarter of an inch wide, and some are curved at the end for dealing with raised bands and corners. Each guppy is set into one wooden handle at will.

c. Guppy (we do not learn his Christian name) is a minor character in Dickens's *Bleak House*. He is the lawyer's clerk, and just one of a number of typically dazzlingly entitled secondary lights, others of whom are called Turveydrop, Krook, Guster and Snagsby.

d. Darko Kerim invites James Bond to join him in some guppy in Ian Fleming's *From Russia with Love*. It seems to be a cross between kedgeree and soup – though the fish is added, and eaten, live. But the vodka that traditionally accompanies such a dish makes them die happy, Darko avers.

---

## You've Read the Book, Now Answer Questions about the Film!

Let's see how lasting and memorable film imagery can be. Below are listed the stars, directors and dates of notable film versions of notable books. But *which* books, that's the point. With authors, please.

1. Joan Fontaine, Orson Welles. Directed by Robert Stevenson, 1943.
2. Richard Attenborough, Hermione Baddeley. Directed by John Boulting, 1947.
3. Richard Burton, Mary Ure. Directed by Tony Richardson, 1959.
4. Sean Connery, Honor Blackman. Directed by Guy Hamilton, 1964.
5. Laurence Olivier, Greer Garson. Directed by Robert Z. Leonard, 1940.
6. Humphrey Bogart, Mary Astor. Directed by John Huston, 1941.

*Answers on page 124*

7. Clark Gable, Vivien Leigh. Directed by Victor Fleming and George Cukor, 1939.
8. Alec Guinness, Robert Newton. Directed by David Lean, 1948.
9. Robert Redford, Mia Farrow. Directed by Jack Clayton, 1974.
10. Laurence Olivier, Merle Oberon. Directed by William Wyler, 1939.

The following works of the 1950s and 1960s were all rather memorably filmed. Who wrote them (with dates, if possible) and just for the dickens of it – who played the leads in the films?

11. *This Sporting Life*
12. *The Entertainer*
13. *Saturday Night and Sunday Morning*
14. *The Loneliness of the Long-Distance Runner*
15. *Room at the Top*
16. *A Taste of Honey*
17. *A Severed Head*
18. *Live Now, Pay Later*
19. *The L-Shaped Room*
20. *A Kind of Loving*

# Quick-Fire Quiz

### Authors' First Books

Sometimes, an author's first book makes their name, and they are for ever best known for it – John Braine's *Room at the Top* comes to mind. This is not always the case, however – indeed, it is not the case with the following list of frightfully famous authors. What we are after here, then, are the titles of their first published works – ten from the nineteenth century, and ten from the twentieth.

1. Charles Dickens
2. Anthony Trollope
3. Thomas Hardy
4. R. L. Stevenson
5. Sir Walter Scott
6. Jerome K. Jerome
7. George Eliot
8. Joseph Conrad
9. George Gissing
10. Wilkie Collins
11. Iris Murdoch
12. John Berger
13. Elizabeth Bowen
14. Angela Carter
15. Scott Fitzgerald
16. E. M. Forster
17. L. P. Hartley
18. James Joyce
19. D. H. Lawrence
20. Anthony Powell

*Answers on page 125*

## Crossword

ACROSS

1. Sounds like the forerunner of pain, but he wrote about that (omitting the first person singular) (6)
5. But this novel was not written by Marcel (3,5)
9. Not Father William – Father Walter! (5)
10. Morgan the work of someone in the rag trade? (6)
11. Resort, or secure (8)
12. Walton loses points for voice (4)
13. Reid team spoiled line through centre (8)
15. Needed by 5, if it comes to a row (4)
17. James did a portrait of one (4)
19. Play by 19, against left (8)
20. Huxley's time must have one (4)
21. Novel's first man – and a venerable one (4,4)
22. A lame one fluffed by Fielding (6)
23. Humpty was, until he cracked (5)
24. The gout's ruined the most Hardy (8)
25. Krushchev – in a kit form! (6)

DOWN

2. Could be a bedouin for the singer Fitzgerald – or a girl for Jude (8)
3. Scattered corps rid parachutists' letdowns (8)
4. Some of Greene's books do this, he says (9)
5. The book's title made no mention of Montmorency (5,3,2,1,4)
6. This Mortimer had digs (7)
7. Vita – in full station (8)
8. Author crashed yachts with hesitation (8)
14. Broken voice not a calling up from the dead (9)

*Solution on page 126*

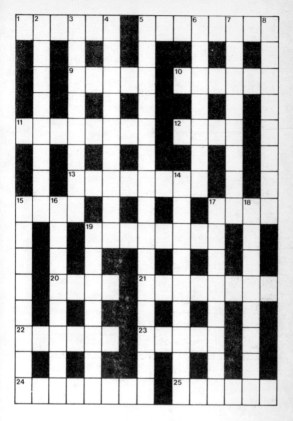

15. Laurence – who went to Khatmandu and
    wrote about Piccadilly! (8)
16. Confessions of he who removed the top of a
    bride's outfit! (8)
17. Bowler's delivery results in injury (3,5)
18. The late Allen Ginsberg, say – down and out
    (4-4)
19. Playwright (French) sounds like boredom (7)

## Acrostic

The first letters of your answers to the cryptic questions will read vertically the name of an author and the title of one of his or her works. Should do, anyway.

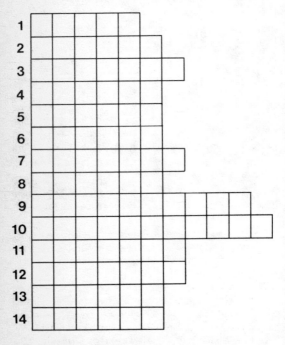

1. King Henry? (5)
2. I, Mars – a sort of musketeer (6)
3. Ghastly Los Angeles lot – I wrote it, he did (7)
4. Waugh Diarist? (6)
5. 'Bennett & Matthew' (6)

*Answers on page 127*

6. More work would be ideal (6)
7. Poet could be last of the big ones (7)
8. Doctor said to go with Rose (6)
9. No end to this dickens of a mystery (5,5)
10. Virginia Woolf on '24 Hours' (5,3,3)
11. Finish grouse, e.g., for Beckett's play (7)
12. Chandler's man – or kit (7)
13. Lupin's Daisy (6)
14. Son of God: that is the author's first name (6)

# Sex

Yes, I know: the book just happened to fall open at this page, and it seemed worth a look. Well, at the risk of this work no longer being classed as good, healthy family entertainment, see if you can identify the following naughty bits. There will be people, you know, who will recognize the lot.

1. I'll come no more behind your scenes, David, for the silk stockings and white bosoms of your actresses excite my amorous propensities.

2. Naked, except for one sock and her charm bracelet, spread-eagled on the bed where my philtre had felled her – so I foreglimpsed her; a velvet hair ribbon was still clutched in her hand; her honey-brown body, with the white negative image of a rudimentary swimsuit patterned against her tan, presented to me its pale breastbuds; in the rosy lamplight, a little pubic floss glistened on its plump hillock.

*Answers on page 127*

3.        Of which mayde anon, maugree hir heed,
          By verray force, he rafte hire maydenhed.

4.    A child's intercourse with anyone responsible for
      his care affords him an unending source of sexual
      excitation and satisfaction from his erotogenic
      zones. This is especially so since the person in
      charge of him, who, after all, is as a rule his mother,
      herself regards him with feelings that are derived
      from her own sexual life: she strokes him, kisses
      him, rocks him and quite clearly treats him as a
      substitute for a complete sexual object. A mother
      would probably be horrified if she were made aware
      that all her marks of affection were rousing her
      child's sexual instinct and preparing for its later
      intensity.

5.    She would fain have cried to him chokingly, held
      out her snowy slender arms to him to come, to feel
      his lips laid on her white brow the cry of a young
      girl's love, a little strangled cry, wrung from her,
      that cry that has rung through the ages. And then a
      rocket sprang and bang shot shot blind and O! then
      the Roman candle burst and it was like a sigh of O!
      and everyone cried O! O! in raptures and it gushed
      out of it a stream of rain gold hair threads and they
      shed and ah! they were all greeny dewy stars falling
      with golden, O so lively! O so soft, sweet, soft!

6.        Sexual intercourse began
          In nineteen sixty-three
          (Which was rather late for me) –
          Between the end of the *Chatterley* ban
          And the Beatles' first LP

7.    'But why don't you now and then try to give me
      pleasure in the act?'
          'I do,' she said, blushing adorably, 'but I don't
      know how to. I've tried to squeeze you, but you
      ravish me and I can only let myself go and throb in
      unison. My feelings are overpowering; every fibre
      in me thrills to you, you great lover.'

**8.**     A man from the *Washington Post*
Once had it off with a ghost;
    At the height of orgasm
    The pale ectoplasm
Shrieked: 'Coming! I'm coming . . . almost!'

**9.**     She put her arms on his shoulders, and with a slightly brutal shove she forced his dark head down on to her bare arm. She hastened with her charge towards the narrow confines of the shadowy realm where she, in her pride, could interpret a moan as an avowal of weakness, and where beggars for favours of her sort drink in the illusion that they are the generous donors.

**10.**     'No, we can't,' she said, in a strong, voluptuous voice of yielding. 'We can only love each other. Say "my love" to me, say it, say it.'

She put her arms round his neck. He enfolded her, and kissed her subtly, murmuring in a subtle voice of love, and irony, and submission: 'Yes – my love, yes – my love. Let love be enough, then. I love you then – I love you. I'm bored by the rest.'

'Yes,' she murmured, nestling very sweet and close to him.

# Quick-Fire Quiz

### Poetical Terminology

Of course one *knows* what all of the following mean, it's just that sometimes one can get them a bit muddled up. And even if one *doesn't* get them muddled up, it can still be tricky to put an explanation into concise, coherent English without padding it out with 'sort of' and 'thingy' and stuttering like a machine-gun; prestige is on offer, then, for the speedy and the succinct. (If, of course,

*Answers on page 131 and 132*

your answers are downright *wrong*, I leave it to your honour to devise a fittingly dreadful punishment; transcribing one hundred lines of Horace springs to mind, and I offer it to you, gratis.)

1. Blank verse
2. Diphthong
3. Caesura
4. Couplet
5. Ode
6. Limerick
7. Haiku
8. Sonnet
9. Shakespearian sonnet
10. Miltonic sonnet
11. Concrete poetry
12. Clerihew
13. Epic

What are the following 'feet'? How many syllables? Where are the stresses?

14. Iambus
15. Anapest
16. Dactyl
17. Spondee
18. Pyrhhic
19. Tribrach
20. Trossachs

## Quick-Fire Quiz

### Pseudonyms

Now, this quiz really isn't very easy at all, because the authors listed below are actually very familiar names indeed, though not one of them is the real thing. I should have thought that if you can uncover *half* of the true identities, you are doing very well indeed. Or maybe you are just naturally nosy.

1. Frank Richards
2. O. Henry
3. James Hadley Chase
4. Henry Green
5. John le Carré
6. B.B.
7. William Cooper
8. Baron Corvo
9. Alice B. Toklas
10. Isak Dinesen
11. Saki
12. Sapper
13. Ross Macdonald
14. Sax Rohmer
15. Flann O'Brien
16. Leslie Charteris
17. Edmund Crispin
18. John Wyndham
19. André Maurois
20. Anthony Burgess

## The 'Double-Devilish' Bookagram

This is a crossword *and* an acrostic, at least. What you do is write in the answers to the cryptic clues

*Answers on page 131 and 132*

in the squares in the grid opposite – *not* in the crossword grid. You then transfer the individual letters from these numbered squares into the correspondingly numbered squares in the crossword grid – this, in turn, should help to suggest answers that you are finding *too* cryptic. The rewards of all this endeavour are as follows: the initial letters of the answers will spell the name of an author and the name of one of his or her works (vertically), and when all the letters of all the answers have been transferred to the crossword grid, you will be able to read – left to right, in the normal way – the opening paragraph of that book, the black squares representing spaces between words.

| | | | | | | | | | | | |
|---|---|---|---|---|---|---|---|---|---|---|---|
| 1 M | ■ | 2 H | 3 I | 4 L | 5 J | 6 C | ■ | 7 G | 8 I | 9 K | 10 I |
| 11 C | 12 K | 13 I | 14 J | ■ | 15 H | 16 H | 17 M | 18 E | 19 G | 20 I | 21 B |
| 22 D | ■ | 23 L | 24 A | 25 I | ■ | 26 K | 27 O | **28 D** | **29 D** | 30 I | 31 N |
| 32 N | 33 M | ■ | 34 H | 35 J | ■ | 36 B | 37 A | 38 O | 39 C | 40 M | 41 L | 42 O |
| 43 B | ■ | 44 F | 45 J | 46 C | 47 N | ■ | 48 O | 49 G | ■ | 50 G | 51 E | 52 F |
| 53 D | 54 O | 55 G | 56 N | ■ | 57 L | 58 O | 59 G | 60 B | ■ | 61 K | ■ | 62 N |
| 63 A | 64 O | ■ | 65 A | 66 H | 67 K | 68 O | 69 A | 70 N | ■ | 71 N | 72 C |
| 73 B | 74 N | 75 L | 76 F | 77 J | 78 G | 79 E | 80 F | ■ | 81 F | 82 E | 83 B |
| 84 K | 85 D | 86 K | ■ | 87 I | 88 M | ■ | 89 J | 90 O | 91 M | 92 C | 93 A |
| 94 C | 95 M | 96 J | ■ | 97 A | 98 G | ■ | 99 N | 100 B | 101 H | ■ | 102 E | 103 K |
| 104 H | 105 A | 106 C | 107 F | 108 M | ■ | 109 B | 110 F | 111 A | 112 G | ■ | 113 M |
| 114 B | 115 D | 116 J | ■ | 117 A | 118 D | 119 I | 120 E | ■ | 121 I | ■ | 122 F | 123 A |
| 124 C | 125 E | 126 O | 127 E | 128 B | 129 O | 130 A | 131 F | 132 J |

A: This has been followed since the year dot (12)
B: As theatrical as Dick Whittington, for instance (10)
C: The journalist who deals with 'the U-boat'? (9)
D: Heaney's work for Scotland? (5)
E: One who decrees raid on NT ruin (8)
F: Writer of 'Log Cabin', it is said (9)
G: What attracted the beast to her? (3,6)
H: Suffered by Eric Idle's spoof group during their film day? (4,3)
I: Term of bunnies and chicks at public school? (6,4)
J: Brazil, for instance – tin RME mess food (9)
K: Feature of Cummings's room (8)
L: Main drink (5)
M: Bandaged ages ago (9)
N: Side value of Rackrent woman (9)
O: Peacock's sort of abbey (11)

| | | | | | | | | | | | | |
|---|---|---|---|---|---|---|---|---|---|---|---|---|
| A | 111 | 24 | 37 | 97 | 105 | 65 | 123 | 63 | 69 | 130 | 117 | 93 |
| B | 73 | 36 | 60 | 43 | 114 | 83 | 100 | 109 | 21 | 128 | | |
| C | 124 | 39 | 94 | 106 | 6 | 11 | 46 | 72 | 92 | | | |
| D | 22 | 85 | 115 | 53 | 118 | | | | | | | |
| E | 18 | 51 | 79 | 82 | 120 | 127 | 102 | 125 | | | | |
| F | 44 | 52 | 122 | 80 | 81 | 131 | 110 | 76 | 107 | | | |
| G | 7 | 112 | 59 | 50 | 55 | 78 | 19 | 98 | 49 | | | |
| H | 2 | 34 | 66 | 101 | 15 | 16 | 104 | | | | | |
| I | 3 | 121 | 13 | 87 | 25 | 20 | 8 | 119 | 30 | 10 | | |
| J | 35 | 77 | 14 | 5 | 45 | 89 | 116 | 132 | 96 | | | |
| K | 9 | 84 | 103 | 12 | 26 | 61 | 86 | 67 | | | | |
| L | 57 | 4 | 23 | 41 | 75 | | | | | | | |
| M | 17 | 95 | 108 | 113 | 1 | 33 | 88 | 91 | 40 | | | |
| N | 31 | 99 | 70 | 74 | 62 | 32 | 56 | 71 | 47 | | | |
| O | 42 | 27 | 38 | 54 | 129 | 48 | 90 | 126 | 68 | 64 | 58 | |

## Scored Lead-On Quiz

The following ten questions have two parts each, and these two parts are in some way connected. Part *a* is supposed to be easy(ish) and Part *b* is supposed to be hardish. They are worth one point and two points, respectively, making a top score of thirty available which, of course, you haven't a blind hope in blazes of attaining. Still, after the answers is an assessment of however many you *do* get. I should be delighted to be proved wrong over the foregoing, incidentally.

1. *a.* Who was Agatha Christie's publisher, virtually throughout her lifetime?
   *b.* Who was Evelyn Waugh's publisher, virtually throughout his lifetime?

2. *a.* Which author lurked under the pseudonym 'Robert Markham' for one book only? And what book, actually?
   *b.* Which author lurked under the pseudonym 'Palinurus' for one book only? And what book was that?

3. *a.* Who wrote *I, Claudius*?
   *b.* Who wrote *I, Claud*?

4. *a.* Who wrote this: 'With the single exception of Homer, there is no eminent writer, not even Sir Walter Scott, whom I can despise so entirely as I despise Shakespeare when I measure my mind against his'?
   *b.* Who was of the opinion that 'Shakespeare never had six lines together without a fault. Perhaps you may find seven, but this does not refute my general assertion'?

*Answers on page 134*

**5.** *a.* Who wrote *Flush*?
   *b.* What is its precise subject matter?

**6.** *a.* Whose first book was *The Sport of Queens*?
   *b.* What, for the author, is singular about this book?

**7.** *a.* *Ariel* – apart from being a volume of poetry by Sylvia Plath – is a 1923 non-fictional work on Shelley. Who wrote it?
   *b.* What is notable about the fact that it was paperbacked?

**8.** *a.* What novel of 1897 is told through the diaries of a young solicitor named Jonathan Harker? And who wrote it?
   *b.* What novel of 1818 (subtitled *The Modern Prometheus*) is told through the letters of an English explorer named Walton? And who wrote it?

**9.** *a.* Who wrote *G*?
   *b.* Who wrote *V*?

**10.** *a.* Who, within a single volume, wrote of characters as diverse as Florence Nightingale, Cardinal Manning, Dr Arnold and General Gordon?
   *b.* And who – also within a single volume – wrote of the following characters, among others: Racine, Sir Thomas Browne, Shakespeare, Voltaire, Rousseau and Blake – and, incidentally, dedicated the volume to John Maynard Keynes?

## Acrostic

Write in the answers to the cryptic posers, and you will be enchanted to discover that the initial letters of these answers will read vertically the name of an author, and the title of one of his or her works.

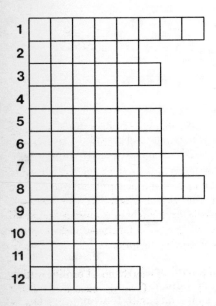

1. Chesterton's man preceded Robinson's man (8)
2. Beckett's days were so contented (5)
3. Goldsmith, or Twist (6)
4. Adams's novel reads: I am a mess (4)
5. Christian name of a writer who is alternatively healthy (6)

*Answers on page 136*

6. In the thirties, writer was in the ascendancy (6)
7. Suggested cloister for Ophelia? (7)
8. Thackeray's *arrivistes*? (8)
9. 'Fabian' was a sort of dance (6)
10. Put back tool, author! (5)
11. Social security perk for Greenwood? (4)
12. Poet, say, and french salad (5)

# Records

One rather hopes you won't know the answers to *any* of these questions, so essentially trivial and indigestible is the whole business of records; still, there is considerable precedent for the allure of trivia, so you might well be sufficiently intrigued to discover the naked truth via the answers. Wallow bogglingly for a while among facts and figures that will instantly fascinate and – I assure you – quite as quickly be forgotten.

1. Who do you think was the most prolific author of all, in terms of words produced? Don't squander the rest of your youth in totting up the likely candidates – the answer's at the back.

2. Some very large amounts of money can be earned by authors these days (or so I'm told) even before a book is published. This is called an advance, and is sometimes made up jointly

*Answers on page 137*

between hardback and paperback publishers, US rights and – occasionally – film option payments. Any idea which lucky fellow has received the *most* money in this way? In Great Britain, that is – we don't want to lose our sense of proportion altogether.

3. Which lady has sold more books – Agatha Christie (who is dead) or Barbara Cartland (who is not only alive, but glamorous and healthy too, as she will keep on reminding us)?

4. And is Agatha Christie the top-selling *crime* novelist of all time? And if you think she isn't, who do you think is?

5. The youngest ever Poet Laureate was only thirty when the honour was bestowed, but have you ever heard of him? If so, what was his name? The greatest age of a poet when made Laureate was seventy-three – and you have most certainly heard of him: name, please.

6. What do you think is the highest price ever paid at auction for a *printed* book? And what book do you suppose it might be?

7. Who wrote the largest number of novels ever?

8. And now, a perfectly straightforward question: which publishing house is the oldest of all?

9. What do you think is the largest print run recorded for a first impression by a *British* publisher? And for what book? And what publisher?

10. Of all the great novels published during the twentieth century, which one do you think has been bought (and, presumably, read) by such vast numbers of people as to render it the all-time bestseller? Think carefully, now.

## The 'Midas' Quiz

Who wrote this clutch of glistering volumes?

1. *The Golden Age*
2. *Jerusalem the Golden*
3. *Good as Gold*
4. *The Golden Ass*
5. *The Golden Child*
6. *The Gold Bat*
7. *The Golden Bough*
8. *The Golden Bowl*
9. *The Golden Notebook*
10. *Realms of Gold*
11. *The Golden Treasury*
12. *Cup of Gold*
13. *The Crock of Gold*
14. *The Man with the Golden Gun*

*Answers on page 140*

## Crossword

ACROSS

1. If there were more than one of this author, lots could be sold (8)
6. 'The fairy slides on the ice' (4)
10. He is concerned with suspicious death (7)
11. His job? Aye, that is the rub (7)
12. Just the ticket, from them (5)
13. Hear the measure of Fleming's boss? (2)
14. Wonder what a metaphysical sounds like (6)
16. Little boat could do this to the heart-strings (3)
17. Greene gave Brontë's man a monkey! (9)
19. Dickens's brothers sound as if they could be made happy (9)
20. Regret what sounds like something from Milne (3)
21. See 4 down
23. Be heard to hesitate over ancient city (2)
24. Dune? A different author (5)
26. To Jeeves, Bertie was much (7)
28. Jean? No, Clarissa (7)
29. A brother for the third man (4)
30. As in black and white (8)


DOWN

2. Raffles his own creation! (7)
3. Pub is gratis to W.B. (9)
4 and 21 across.  The years of the prayer's days of our age (5,5,3,3)
5. Tree took leading part in *Elmer Gantry* (3)
6. Alphabetically, Italian food is 'B' (5)
7. American writer for revolutionary, for ever (7)
8. Tax sounds like Walter (4)

*Solution on page 141*

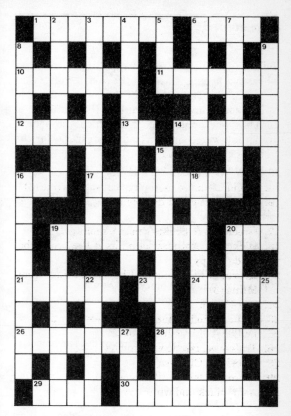

9. We have heard that this novelist is a worth-
   less woman (8)
15. You have this when you join the politician's
    joint (10)
16. The protagonist in *Death in the Afternoon*? (8)
18. He's in 'The Bull' for the lexicon (9)
19. *La petite fille* hasn't got one. *Le garçon* has (7)
20. Not hunting pink, but a British soldier (7)
22. But marbles aren't from a Scottish town! (5)
25. Chicken, to his friends at Christmas (4)
27. Ode rewritten to God (3)

## Clichés

Below are listed some appallingly familiar phrases and exhortations – the sort of things that schoolchildren and would-be authors are urged to avoid; some have even acquired the status (?) of maxims and aphorisms. It is difficult to believe that they were once written down fresh, for the very first time – and sometimes by some rather surprising people. Who, actually?

1. All Hell broke loose
2. Hail fellow, well met
3. Abandon all hope, you who enter!
4. Accidents will occur
5. Answer came there none
6. The law is a ass
7. I have it here in black and white
8. Blessings in disguise
9. Boys will be boys
10. Cloudcuckooland
11. The course of true love never did run smooth
12. To err is human, to forgive divine
13. What's done is done
14. East is east, and west is west, and never the twain shall meet
15. The female of the species is more deadly than the male
16.       'Tis better to have loved and lost, Than never to have loved at all
17. Eureka!
18. If music be the food of love, play on
19. Money is the root of all evil
20. Funny peculiar or funny-ha-ha?

*Answers on page 142*

## Book Collecting

Although the above heading might put off one or
two, the questions also concern the business of the
physical book, which should be of more than passing interest. One or two of the answers, I modest-
ly venture, might even prove to be illuminating.

1. *a.* What is a 'collected author'?
   *b.* If, in a bookseller's catalogue, you come
       across the term 'collected set' (referring to
       a group of books) and later on a reference to
       a 'collected edition', would you take them
       to mean the same? And if so, what do they
       mean? And if not, what do they mean?

2. If the following *first* editions were to come up
   at auction, roughly what prices (all right –
   *very* roughly) would you expect them to command?:

   *a.* *Robinson Crusoe* (Daniel Defoe, 1719)
   *b.* *Jane Eyre* (Charlotte Brontë, 1847)
   *c.* *Ivanhoe* (Walter Scott, 1819)
   *d.* *Poems* (W. H. Auden, 1928)
   *e.* The Gutenberg Bible (1453–5)
   *f.* *Saint Joan* (Bernard Shaw, 1924)
   *g.* *The Mysterious Affair at Styles* (Agatha
       Christie, 1920)
   *h.* *Frankenstein* (Mary Shelley, 1818)
   *i.* *Winnie-the-Pooh* (A. A. Milne, 1926)
   *j.* *Lord of the Flies* (William Golding, 1954)
   *k.* *Midnight's Children* (Salman Rushdie,
       1981)
   *l.* *Watership Down* (Richard Adams, 1972)

*Answers on page 143*

3. *a.* If a fellow says he collects 'modern first editions', what do you suppose is meant by 'modern'?

   *b.* And if another fellow boasts of his array of 'early printed' books, what do you consider is meant by 'early'?

4. The following acronyms are used by booksellers in their catalogues, and if one is hoping to know what on earth they are talking about, it is as well to understand them. Do *you* understand them?

   *a.* D/W
   *b.* T/P
   *c.* E/P
   *d.* O/P
   *e.* VGC
   *f.* AEG
   *g.* WAF
   *h.* TLS

5. *a.* What is a book that has been 'Bowdlerized'?

   *b.* What is a book that has been 'Grangerized'?

6. If I give you a clue and tell you that a 'three-decker' is *not* an inordinately tall London bus, could you opine what on earth it might be?

7. *a.* What is meant when the pages of an antiquarian book are said to be 'unopened'?

   *b.* 'Uncut' means the same. Yes? No?

8. When do you suppose the paper dust-wrapper (or dust jacket, as such people as publishers will call it) first made its appearance? Does the presence of the thing notably affect the value of a first edition, do you think? Or is it

just the condition of the book itself and the presence of all plates that determine the value?

9. Illustrated books have long been collected for the illustrations themselves – sometimes regardless of the text, although the perfect marriage of the two is seen to be ideal. Such as Arthur Rackham, Edmund Dulac, Walter Crane, Maxfield Parrish and Kay Nielsen have their devotees, as do artists like Eric Ravilious, Edward Bawden, Frank Brangwyn, Gwen Raverat and Robert Gibbings. Most of these people, of course, were illustrating already established texts – Shakespeare, children's classics, modern works of literature and so on. Some books, though, were illustrated on first publication, and the illustrations are now seen to be inseparable from the texts. Such are those listed below. Illustrators, please – and authors.

   *a. Winnie-the-Pooh*
   *b. Alice's Adventures in Wonderland*
   *c. The Hobbit*
   *d.* The *William* books
   *e.* The *Sherlock Holmes* stories
   *f. The Twits*
   *g. Old Possum's Book of Practical Cats*
   *h. The Wind in the Willows*
   *i. In His Own Write*
   *j.* The *Grey Rabbit* books

10. The truth can now be told! Some people *do* collect books just for the bindings; odd leather bindings which look quite nice, and the contents of which are dire (sermons and tracts, usually, by fusty clergymen now long since reverted to dust and ashes), are referred to in the trade as 'furniture'. They sell to interior

designers: books really *do* furnish a room. Now, if everyone has recovered from this onslaught to their sensibilities, we shall talk of *real* books in *real* bindings – that is, creditable texts (not by any means necessarily first editions) well printed on good paper in a unique binding created by hand, as opposed to an all-in-one cover slapped on by a machine, replete with hollow and fake raised bands on the spine. Here are a few questions about *the real thing*.

*a.* Those raised bands alluded to above – the handsome ridges (usually five) on the spine of a binding. Why are they there? Just for the look of the thing?

*b.* What is a *full* binding? A *half*-binding? A *quarter*-binding?

*c.* Any idea what a 'fore-edge painting' might be?

*d.* Why is the top edge of a book often gilded, or coloured? And why is the gilding sometimes applied to all three edges?

*e.* Have you ever heard of a Solander Case? What might it be?

## True or False?

Now, as you have a fifty-fifty chance on these little posers, I think that it is only fair that I ask you to answer them *quickly*. And I should be greatly obliged for *reasons* as to why you came down on the side you did.

1. P. G. Wodehouse, Agatha Christie and Georges Simenon all published over one hundred books each?
2. Joseph Conrad's true surname is 'Korzeniowski'?
3. Dante was born in 1465?
4. In *Oliver Twist*, Fagin's Christian name (if that's the term I want) was Samuel?
5. P. D. James is Margaret Drabble's sister?
6. 'Sans wine, sans song, sans singer, and – sans end!' is a quotation from *As You Like It*?
7. Chaucer's *Canterbury Tales* comprise twenty-four stories?
8. 'Runcible Cat with Crimson Whiskers' failed to make the transfer from Eliot's *Old Possum* to the musical *Cats*?
9. Allen Lane's original intention, in 1935, was that his new imprint should be called 'Falcon Books', but he was persuaded into the more friendly and gentle image of the penguin?
10. In the first (1775) edition of his Dictionary, Johnson (in his role as 'harmless drudge') defined 'network' thus: 'Anything reticulated or decussated, at equal distances, with interstices between the intersections'?
11. What James Bond drank more than anything was a vodka-martini, shaken not stirred?
12. George Orwell's *Animal Farm* was turned down by T. S. Eliot at Faber, before being accepted by Secker & Warburg?

*Answers on page 151*

13. Hardy never wrote another novel after *Jude the Obscure*, very largely because he was shocked and hurt by critical reaction?

14. Proust was not, in fact, French, but Belgian with a faint strain of Corsican?

15. Shaw said: 'I am not given to seeing anything of me in the characters that people my plays – but I suppose there is a touch of Dubedat, if anyone at all; more, anyway, than any other'?

16. In all the Sherlock Holmes long and short stories, the great detective uttered 'Elementary, my dear Watson' only twice?

17. *'Tis Pity She's a Whore* was written by John Webster, and printed in 1633?

18. Winston Churchill's *History of the Second World War* was a six-volume work, and his *History of the English-Speaking Peoples* was a four-volume work?

19. Cyril Connolly wrote just one novel, but it has yet to be published?

20. Beatrix Potter is on record as having confided that she 'quite hates Peter Rabbit. He rather scares me'?

## Acrostic

Just answer the cryptic clues, and then discover to your amazement that the initial letters of those answers, when read vertically, will reveal the name of an author, followed by the title of one of his or her works.

1. Bathsheba always swift, I hear (8)
2. Scrap no limit – but leave one out for poet (6)

*Answers on page 153*

3. Murdoch's flag (4)
4. It's Green's – being very affectionate (6)
5. Christie's night was like a circle (7)
6. MacNeice's menagerie (3)
7. You can't get this sort of book (3,2,5)
8. Hardy's lukewarm work (9)
9. Classically, she went to *terra mirabilis* (7)
10. Novel – Gissing's sort of Grub Street (3)
11. Writer's ruined our hat (6)
12. Twist character in annan cycle (5)
13. A right Kingsley character in Dumas! (6)

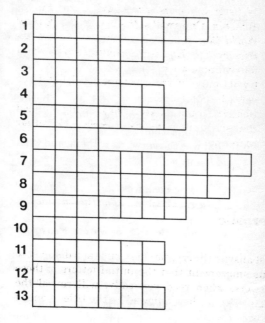

## Scored Lead-On Quiz

With this quiz, the answers are rather longer and
more involved than the questions – if you want
them to be. The format relies upon ten questions,
however – each of two connected parts; part *a* is
not *too* difficult, and part *b* is not exactly easy, and
you – the impartial scorer – award yourself *one*
point for a correct part *a*, and *two* points for a
correct part *b*. As I say, the answers can be fuller
and more rewarding than the questions might
appear to imply, so I leave it to your integrity to be
true unto yourself, so that you won't hate yourself
in the morning. Catches may or may not abound.

1. *a.* Who wrote *Casanova*?
   *b.* Who wrote *Don Juan*?

2. *a.* In which periodical did the Sherlock
      Holmes stories *usually* appear, prior to
      book publication?
   *b.* What was the very first of them, and where
      did *it* appear?

3. *a.* Whose first book was *Call from the Dead*?
   *b.* Whose first book was *The Biafra Story*?

4. *a.* Who wrote *Pamela, or Virtue Rewarded*?
      When-ish?
   *b.* Who wrote *Shamela Andrews*? When-ish?

5. *a.* What have the following in common:
      Dryden, Southey, Wordsworth, Tennyson?
   *b.* What have the following in common: Luigi
      Pirandello, Eugene O'Neill, Samuel Beck-
      ett, Jean-Paul Sartre?

*Answers on page 153*

6.  *a.* Bernard Shaw was well established as a journalist and critic when, at the age of thirty-six, his first play was produced. Title? Date?

  *b.* And what was Shakespeare's first play? When was it published?

7.  *a.* What do the following novels have in common: *The Moving Finger, The Mirror Crack'd from Side to Side, The Pale Horse, By the Pricking of My Thumbs*?

  *b.* What *else* do they have in common?

8.  *a.* Proust's *À la recherche du temps perdu* was first published between 1913 and 1927 in France, the English translation appearing from 1922 until 1931. What was the English title? Who translated it? And who revised that translation for the new edition of 1981?

  *b.* Although the first English edition was published in twelve slimmish volumes, and the 1981 edition in three fat ones, the French original was done in seven parts, and I should like the titles of these seven parts that make up the whole – in English, in order to render it simple.

9.  *a.* With which author do you associate the word 'Metroland'?

  *b.* With which *other* author do you associate the word 'Metroland'?

10.  *a.* To date, Martin Amis has published five novels. Name them, in order.

  *b.* Odd that this should be tougher, but I now want (you guessed it) the first five novels, in order, of *Kingsley* Amis. (*Novels*, I emphasize.)

## Quick-Fire Quiz

### Household 'Name' Reference Books

It is seen to be rather stylish in bookish circles to refer to a standard work by the surname of the author or editor of the thing (or, even, in a few cases, the publisher) rather than by its far more enlightening title, and this is never more true than with works of reference. Such is elitism. If someone doesn't know what is meant, they have no business opening their mouths – or, indeed, breathing at all. You, of course, *will* know what is meant. What sort of specialist information is one after if one looks something up in . . .

1. Pevsner
2. Baedeker
3. Godden
4. Fowler
5. Johnson
6. Brewer
7. Kobbé
8. Roget
9. Benezit
10. Partridge
11. Palgrave
12. Bannister-Fletcher
13. Wisden
14. Bean
15. Harvey
16. Gombrich
17. Debrett
18. Groves
19. Whitaker
20. Freud

## Author Identification

There follow the opening lines of fifteen twentieth-century novels, and, naturally enough, I am seeking the authors and the titles. And just to help you on your way, I am *giving* you the authors, though

*Answers on page 161 and 162*

in a scrambled order. All that is required, then, is the matching of the author with the opening (easy, you would think, with a list containing such divers creatures as P. G. Wodehouse and Norman Mailer), and, of course, if you can identify the actual book as well, this is so much more to the good.

*The Authors*

a.  D. H. Lawrence
b.  Dick Francis
c.  Norman Mailer
d.  Lawrence Durrell
e.  Graham Greene
f.  Colin Wilson
g.  Ernest Hemingway
h.  Muriel Spark
i.  Iris Murdoch
j.  Kingsley Amis
k.  Ian Fleming
l.  C. P. Snow
m.  Len Deighton
n.  P. G. Wodehouse
o.  Frederick Forsyth

*The Openings*

1.  Of the three men at the table, all dressed in black business suits, two must have been stone drunk. Not Nash, the reproachful, of course not. But Vibart the publisher (of late all too frequently): and then Your Humble, Charlock, the thinking weed: on the run again. Felix Charlock, at your service. Your humble, Ma'am.

2.  They started two hours before daylight, and at first, it was not necessary to break the ice across the canal as other boats had gone ahead. In each boat, in the darkness, so you could not see, but only hear him, the poler stood in the stern, with his long oar.

**3.** Punctually at six o'clock the sun set with a last yellow flash behind the Blue Mountains, a wave of violet shadow poured down Richmond Road, and the crickets and tree frogs in the fine gardens began to zing and tingle.

**4.** Fanny Peronett was dead. That much her husband Hugh Peronett was certain of as he stood in the rain beside the grave which was shortly to receive his wife's mortal remains. Further than that, Hugh's certainty did not reach.

**5.** It was the morning of my hundredth birthday. I shaved the final mirror-disc of old tired face under the merciless glare of the bathroom lighting. It was all very well telling oneself that Humphrey Bogart had that sort of face; but he also had a hairpiece, half a million dollars a year and a stand-in for the rough bits.

**6.** The Commissioner was careful of his appearance before meeting men younger than himself. It gave him the same kind of confidence as dressing for dinner had done in eastern forests.

**7.** The sunshine which is such an agreeable feature of life in and around Hollywood, when the weather is not unusual, blazed down from a sky of turquoise blue on the spacious grounds of what, though the tempestuous Mexican star had ceased for nearly a year to be its owner and it was now the property of Mrs Adela Shannon Cork, was still known locally as Carmen Flores place. The month was May, the hour noon.

**8.** There was a God-awful cock-up in Bologna.

**9.** It was the Sunday after Easter, and the last bull-fight of the season in Mexico City. Four special bulls had been brought over from Spain for the occasion, since Spanish bulls are more fiery than Mexican. Perhaps it is the altitude, perhaps just the spirit of the western Continent which is to blame for the lack of 'pep', as Owen put it, in the native animal.

10.    There were no stars that night on the bush air-strip, nor any moon; just the West African darkness wrapping round the scattered groups like warm, wet velvet. The cloud cover was lying hardly off the tops of the iroko trees and the waiting men prayed it would stay a while longer to shield them from the bombers.

11.    As the taxi turned the corner at Shepherd's Bush, the first flakes of snow drifted against the window. Before they were halfway to Notting Hill, it was snowing so heavily that visibility was limited to a few yards.

'I thought so. Been expectin' this all day. Either that or rain.'

Professor Karl Zweig did not reply – not because he disliked the driver's familiarity, but because he could think of nothing to say.

12.    As the car passed the first houses away from London Airport (the September night had closed down, lights shone from windows, in the back seat one heard the grinding of the windscreen wiper) Margaret said:

'Is there anything waiting for us?'

'I hope not.'

She meant bad news. It was the end of a journey, the end of a holiday, coming home.

13.    The sheep clustered by the infant oak-tree looked up suddenly and turned their heads. Something was coming towards them over the close-cropped turf, coming fast. At the same time a low noise that might have been the beginning of a storm grew steadily louder, and there seemed to be a vibration underfoot. The sheep swung abruptly aside and started to run.

14.    In the cactus wild of Southern California, a distance of two hundred miles from the capital of cinema, as I choose to call it, is the town of Desert d'Or. There I went from the Air Force to look for a good time. Some time ago.

15. He was driving along the road in France from St Die to Nancy in the district of Meurtle; it was straight and almost white, through thick woods of fir and birch. He came to the grass track on the right that he was looking for. It wasn't what he expected. Nothing ever is, he thought.

## Odd One Out

Which member of each of the following groups does not belong? The odds are fairly good if you just guess – but where is the satisfaction in that? You really must know *why*, otherwise it's silly for both of us.

1. Adrian Henri, Roger McGough, Adrian Mitchell, Brian Patten
2. W. B. Yeats, G. B. Shaw, T. S. Eliot, W. H. Auden
3. Leslie Stephen, Vanessa Bell, Virginia Woolf, Lytton Strachey
4. *The Adventures of Roderick Random*, *Jorrocks's Jaunts and Jollities*, *The Adventures of Peregrine Pickle*, *The Expedition of Humphry Clinker*
5. The Left Book Club, Collins Crime Club, The Book-of-the-Month Club, The Folio Society
6. George Sand, George Eliot, George Orwell, George Bernard Shaw
7. *Janine 1982, 1983, 1984, 1985*
8. Salman Rushdie, Ruth Prawer Jhabvala, Shiva Naipaul, J. G. Farrell
9. Mr Polly, Mr Norris, Mrs Gaskell, Mrs Dalloway
10. Nugent, Wharton, Berry, Hurree Jamset Ram Singh

*Answers on page 162*

# Quick-Fire Quiz

### Characters in Series

The following characters have appeared in more than one (usually *many* more than one) work by the same author: names of the series, and names of the writers, please.

1. Felix Leiter
2. Lord Mauleverer
3. Widmerpool
4. Horatio Stubbs
5. Grabber
6. Mycroft
7. Jane
8. Violet Elizabeth
9. Venables
10. M'Turk
11. Mr Plod
12. The Empress
13. Crouchback
14. Algy
15. Algy Pug
16. Smiley
17. Lewis Eliot
18. Commander Caractatus Potts
19. Aunt Agatha
20. Harry Palmer

*Answers on page 165*

## Crossword

ACROSS

1. Take it as read (10)
9. Wake up a Shakespearian scholar, say (6)
10. One of Stoppard's disguises (8)
11. A couple of pounds, 'e is rich (spoiled German writer) (8)
12. Auden paid his homage to the muse (4)
13. James wrote of one of these (9)
16. Controversial lip – come! (7)
18. Dug up root in a province (7)
21. A Brontë? (5,4)
22. Money! Success! He has done them all (4)
24. He's for king (8)
27. Rain-dues ruined water-god (8)
28. Make evident point to small Van Gogh (6)
29. She's taking care of business (10)

DOWN

2. In front of Russian orders – Japanese seal (4)
3. A necessity for a man of letters? (8)
4. Patrick White was one (10)
5. This book has a bloom (7)
6. Per Everyman (4)
7. Joyce's city-dweller (8)
8. Lady much addressed by G.B.S. (5)
12. Publisher's cloak (4)
14. This author had an agent (3,7)
15. Gentlemen aspire to the light-headed, she said (4)
17. The other 22's fortunate fellow (5,3)
18. First name of Gray – he wrote unlikely stories, mostly (8)

*Solution on page 167*

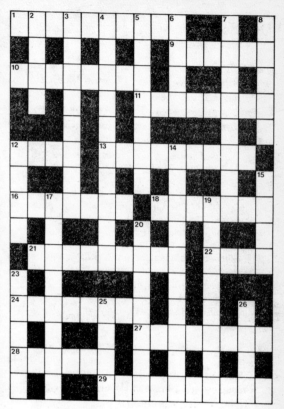

20. Tom Jones character in a cowboy film? (7)
23. Loving, wrote Henry: naïve (5)
25. In Latin, same . . . (4)
26. . . . Question answered by 'the egotist'? (4)

## Detectives

There follow the opening lines of ten very famous works of detective fiction. I should like a stab at the author, if not the actual book – though this, of course, would be ideal. Each book, by the way, is by a *different* author, and I am not at all sure whether that makes it harder or not.

1.   It began on a summer's morning in July. The sun came up early in the morning mist, and the pavements were already steaming a little from the heavy dew. The air in the streets was stale and lifeless. It had been an exhausting month of intense heat, rainless skies, and warm, dust-laden winds.

2.   Between what matters and what seems to matter, how should the world we know judge wisely?
     When the scheming, indomitable brain of Sigsbee Manderson was scattered by a shot from an unknown hand, that world lost nothing worth a single tear.

3.   In the month of December 1918, and on the very day that a British Cavalry Division marched into Cologne, with flags flying and bands playing as the conquerors of a beaten nation, the manager of the Hotel Nationale in Berne received a letter. Its contents appeared to puzzle him somewhat, for having read it twice he rang the bell on his desk to summon his secretary.

4.   The scene is a bedroom in Sudeley Hall preparatory school: not one of the airy, green-washed, ostentatiously hygienic dormitories so reassuring to the science-ridden mind of modern parenthood; but one of those bedrooms resembling in its extreme narrowness and draughtiness nothing so much as a section of corridor in an express train, which tradition assigns to dons, schoolmasters and the lower ranks of domestic servant.

*Answers on page 168*

**5.**     Mrs Ferrars died on the night of the 16th–17th September – a Thursday. I was sent for at eight o'clock on the morning of Friday the 17th. There was nothing to be done. She had been dead some hours.

**6.**     The first time I laid eyes on Terry Lennox he was drunk in a Rolls Royce Silver Wraith outside the terrace of The Dancers. The parking lot attendant had brought the car out and he was still holding the door open because Terry Lennox's left foot was still dangling outside, as if he had forgotten he had one.

**7.**     Harriet Vane sat at her writing table, and stared out into Mecklenburg Square. The late tulips made a brave show in the Square garden, and a quartet of early tennis players were energetically calling the score of a rather erratic and unpractised game.

**8.**     An academic life, Dr Johnson observed, puts one little in the way of extraordinary casualties. This was not the experience of the Fellows and scholars of St Anthony's College when they awoke one raw November morning to find their President, Josiah Umpleby, murdered in the night.

**9.**     In the year 1878 I took my degree of Doctor of Medicine of the University of London, and proceeded to Netley to go through the course prescribed for surgeons in the army. Having completed my studies there, I was duly attached to the Fifth Northumberland Fusiliers as Assistant Surgeon.

**10.**     Between the silver ribbon of morning and the green glittering ribbon of sea, the boat touched Harwich and let loose a swarm of folk like flies, among whom the man we must follow was by no means conspicuous – nor wished to be.

## Quick-Fire Quiz

### Authors and Characters

A hotch-potch of questions about people's names, this time – authors as well as characters in their works. Quite easy, this lot – so try to move *faster*.

1. What was the name of Sherlock Holmes's housekeeper?
2. What was Jeeves's Christian name?
3. Who was the simple boy befriended by Nicholas Nickleby?
4. Who wrote detective novels under the name of Nicholas Blake?
5. The Christian name of *Mrs* Charles Pooter?
6. Who called whom 'nuncle'?
7. Acton, Currer and Ellis Bell were pseudonyms adopted by the Brontë sisters. Which was which?
8. Who is the protagonist in *1984*?
9. And who in *Crime and Punishment*?
10. Who was Mrs Piozzi?
11. One of the would-be democrats in *Lord of the Flies* is called Ralph. What is the name of the other?
12. In Sheridan's *The Rivals*, who is Lydia Languish's aunt?

What do the following initials stand for?

13. J. G. Ballard
14. W. S. Gilbert
15. C. V. Wedgwood
16. W. B. Yeats
17. A. S. Byatt
18. M. R. James
19. P. D. James
20. P. G. Wodehouse

*Answers on page 168*

# The Grand General Book Quiz

These questions dot about all over the place. It keeps you on your toes.

1. Edgar Wallace's *The Four Just Men* was published by the Tallis Press in 1905. This publishing house consisted of just one room in Temple Chambers, London, owned and run almost singlehandedly by Wallace himself. What else – apart from the subsequent fame of the book – was singular about its publication?

2. –––– in his edition undoubtedly did many things wrong, and left many things undone; but let him not be defrauded of his due praise. He was the first that knew, at least the first that told, by what helps the text might be improved. If he inspected the early editions negligently, he taught others to be more accurate.

   Who is discussing whose edition of what?

3. Who might have written (in a personal letter dated 6 April 1958), 'the new Ian Fleming, *Dr No*, is pretty poor: after a brilliant opening chapter, the whole story becomes so improbable that, although his narrative gift makes one read on, unbelief is not for a moment suspended'?

4. What do you think is being discussed here, and by whom?

   a. Everything has gone from me but the certainty of your goodness. I cant go on spoiling your life any longer. I dont think two people could have been happier than we were.

   b. It is a decision I shall not take, at least not yet, for the reason that I have got myself annuities

*Answers on page 170*

from two sovereigns and I should be inconsolable if my death enriched two crowned heads.

    *c.*    Done because we are too menny.

5. April the 23rd – as any right-thinking Englishman is well aware – is St George's Day. What else is it?

6. Who are writing about themselves?
    *a.*    With Sean O'Casey's statement that I am English Literature's performing flea I scarcely know how to deal. Thinking it over, I believe he meant to be complimentary, for all the performing fleas I have met have impressed me with their sterling artistry and that indefinable something which makes the good trouper.

    *b.*    With sixty staring me in the face, I have developed inflammation of the sentence structure and a definite hardening of the paragraphs.

    *c.*    I think I may claim to have been, for the first twenty years of my career, the best abused author in England. Punch invariably referred to me as 'Arry K.'Arry, and would then proceed to solemnly lecture me on the sin of mistaking vulgarity for humour and impertinence for wit.

    *d.*    Twenty-four years ago, Madam, I was incredibly handsome. The remains of it are still visible through the rift of time. I was so handsome that women became spellbound when I came in view. In San Francisco, in rainy seasons, I was frequently mistaken for a cloudless day.

    *e.*    What I write in a hurry I always feel to be not worth reading, and what I try to take pains with, I am sure never to finish . . .

7. Max Beerbohm published his only completed novel in 1911 – *Zuleika Dobson*. In what year did *The Works of Max Beerbohm* appear, how many volumes did it run to, and what was singular about its publication?

8. Who was of the opinion that 'the English have no respect for their language, and will not teach their children to speak it'?

    And who seemed to take him at his word and wrote the following: 'Ow, eez ye-ooa san, is e? Wal, fewd dan y'de-ooty bawmz a mather should, eed now bettern to spawl a pore gel's flahrzn than ran away athaht pyin.'?

9. Who exhorted us to 'eat, drink and be merry'?

10. Who on earth *is* this young lady?

    My name is Vivienne Michel and, at the time, I was sitting in the Dreamy Pines motel and re-membering. I was twenty-three. I am five feet six, and I always thought I had a good figure until the English girls at Astor House told me my behind stuck out too much and that I must wear a tighter bra.

11. Is Anthony Powell's *A Dance to the Music of Time* his own invented title? Or is it a quotation? Or what is it?

12. Sometimes, we contract the titles of books. No one (perhaps excusably) talks of *The Posthumous Papers of the Pickwick Club*; more maddeningly, people *never* precede *Lear* with *King*, nor follow *Brideshead* with *Revisited*. On the other hand, some books we know only by their abbreviated titles, the full thing sometimes running on for lines. Any idea what very well-known works follow these preambles, or lurk within the contractions?

    a. *The Life and Strange and Surprising Adventures of* . . .
    b. *The Strange Case of* . . .
    c. *The History of* . . . . . . . . . *, a Foundling*
    d. . . . . . . . . . *, a Pure Woman*
    e. *The Expedition of* . . .

    f. *The Fortunes and Misfortunes of the Famous* ...
    g. *The Life and Opinions of* ...
    h. *... , the Sacred and Profane Memories of Captain Charles Ryder*
    i. *... , or, What You Will*

13. Who wrote:

> T. S. Eliot is quite at a loss
> When clubwomen bustle across
>     At literary teas
>     Crying, 'What, if you please,
> Did you mean by *The Mill on the Floss?*'

14. What the blazes is *honorificabilitudinitatibus?*

15. English titles, please – and authors – of the following:

    a. *Lé Blé en herbe*
    b. *L'Étranger*
    c. *Huis clos*
    d. *Lá Porte étroite*
    e. *Die Blechtrommel*

16. Who edited the following Oxford anthologies?

    a. *The Oxford Book of English Verse 1250–1918*
    b. *The New Oxford Book of English Verse 1250–1950*
    c. *The Oxford Book of Light Verse*
    d. *The New Oxford Book of Light Verse*
    e. *The Oxford Book of Modern Verse 1892–1935*
    f. *The Oxford Book of Twentieth-Century Verse*
    g. *The Oxford Book of Contemporary Verse 1945–1980*
    h. *The Oxford Book of Children's Verse*

    *i.*  *The Oxford Book of Satirical Verse*
    *j.*  *The Oxford Book of War Poetry*

17. What does Jeeves have in common with Bunter?

    And what does Georges Simenon have in common with Hercule Poirot?

18. Who are the authors responsible for the spectrum?

    *a.*  *The Rose Tattoo*
    *b.*  *Prater Violet*
    *c.*  *Porterhouse Blue*
    *d.*  *Ultramarine*
    *e.*  *Green Mansions*
    *f.*  *The Yellowplush Papers*
    *g.*  *A Clockwork Orange*
    *h.*  *Redgauntlet*
    *i.*  *A Study in Scarlet*
    *j.*  *Vermilion Sands*
    *k.*  *Gravity's Rainbow*

19. Can any sense whatever be made of the following?

    *a.*  Son-in-law
    *b.*  Can! I am new!
    *c.*  Real Hindu mass
    *d.*  Is ram a mint?
    *e.*  Near book train

20. What is the common denominator for the following: Thomas Chatterton, Virginia Woolf, Sylvia Plath, Arthur Koestler, John Berryman?

**21.** Below are listed ten authors, and ten post-war novels. Can you match them up?

| | | | |
|---|---|---|---|
| a. | Penelope Fitzgerald | 1. | *The Dressmaker* |
| b. | C. P. Snow | 2. | *The Scarperer* |
| c. | Beryl Bainbridge | 3. | *The Victim* |
| d. | L. P. Hartley | 4. | *The Hollow* |
| e. | Philip Roth | 5. | *The Millstone* |
| f. | Agatha Christie | 6. | *The Bookshop* |
| g. | Brendan Behan | 7. | *The Boat* |
| h. | Saul Bellow | 8. | *The Unicorn* |
| i. | Iris Murdoch | 9. | *The Breast* |
| j. | Margaret Drabble | 10. | *The Affair* |

**22.** Below are listed ten poets, and ten post-war slim volumes. Can you match them up?

| | | | |
|---|---|---|---|
| a. | John Berryman | 1. | *The Age of Anxiety* |
| b. | Siegfried Sassoon | 2. | *Love and Fame* |
| c. | Thom Gunn | 3. | *High and Low* |
| d. | Robert Lowell | 4. | *On Seeming to Presume* |
| e. | W. H. Auden | 5. | *Fighting Terms* |
| f. | Ezra Pound | 6. | *Wintering Out* |
| g. | John Betjeman | 7. | *Near the Ocean* |
| h. | Seamus Heaney | 8. | *Holes in the Sky* |
| i. | Lawrence Durrell | 9. | *Thrones* |
| j. | Louis MacNeice | 10. | *Sequences* |

**23.** What are the first names of the following authors? Nothing simpler, you would think.

a. Kipling
b. Woolf
c. Beerbohm
d. Bennett (the *Riceyman Steps* fellow)
e. Brontë (the brother)
f. Firbank
g. Lewis (the *Elmer Gantry* man)
h. Lowry
i. Potter (she of *Peter Rabbit*)

    *j.* Strachey
    *k.* Wallace
    *l.* Colette

24. And finally, questions 'one to ten'. Who wrote:

    *a. One of Our Conquerors*
    *b. Two is Lonely*
    *c. Threepenny Novel*
    *d. Four Quartets*
    *e. The Five Red Herrings*
    *f. Six Characters in Search of an Author*
    *g. Seven Types of Ambiguity*
    *h. When Eight Bells Toll*
    *i. The Nine Tailors*
    *j. Ten Little Niggers*

---

# The Penguin Fiftieth Birthday Quiz

Now here at last is a quiz actually *worth* spending your time on: *prizes!* (See Publisher's Note at the end of the quiz.)

1. In what year did the first Pelican appear? What was its title? And (apart from its being the first Pelican) what made it unique in the Penguin list?

2. In 1939, Penguin published its first hardcover book as the forerunner of a series. What was the title of the book, and what was the title of the series? And for what other reason was this a Penguin 'first'?

3. What *two* factors are significant about the publication of *The Puffin Song Book* in 1956?

4. In 1944, the *Penguin Modern Painters* series was launched, in landscape format, and with colour plates. Which of the following painters were *not* included in the series: David Jones, Vanessa Bell, Augustus John, Duncan Grant, Ivon Hitchens, Paul Klee, Henri Matisse, Pablo Picasso, Edward Burra, Ben Shahn, David Bomberg?

5. In the early days, colour coding of Penguin covers was used to denote the category of book, orange being the most famous for fiction. What did the following colours signify?

   *a.* green
   *b.* light blue
   *c.* dark blue
   *d.* cerise
   *e.* red
   *f.* yellow

6. Who designed the Penguin symbol currently in use as a colophon at the base of the spine of Penguin fiction and non-fiction? And when did it first make its appearance?

7. Why was the publication of the following two titles (in 1946 and 1951, respectively) so significant?

   *a.* *The Odyssey*
   *b.* *Cornwall*

8. What do the following artists have in common – with special reference to Penguin: Helen Bunyan, Gwen Raverat, Douglas P. Bliss, Robert Gibbings, Ethelbert White, Ian MacNab, J. R. Biggs, Gertrude Hermes, Theodore Nash?

9. What were 'Ptarmigans'?

10. Who was the designer largely responsible for Penguin abandoning their typography-only covers in the 1960s, and who introduced brightly coloured graphics and artwork?

11. Which book – a Penguin for very many years, and still in print – ends, rather suitably, thus:

    For we are a nation of shopkeepers, and no shop-keeper will look at research which does not promise him a financial return within a year. And so you will sledge nearly alone, but those with whom you sledge will not be shopkeepers: that is worth a good deal. If you march your Winter Journeys you will have your reward, so long as all you want is a penguin's egg.

    And what was significant about its first Penguin appearance?

12. George Bernard Shaw, H. G. Wells, Evelyn Waugh, Agatha Christie, D. H. Lawrence.
    This unlikely flock of Penguin authors is brought together by one publishing accolade unique to Penguin. What is it?

13. Name in each case the one work of *fiction* published:
    *a.* as a Penguin Special
    *b.* as a Pelican

14. What do the Penguin editions of Daudet's *Letters from My Windmill*, Eleanor Farjeon's *The Little Bookroom* and Graham Greene's *The Little Train* have in common?

**15.** Penguin has often, but not always, celebrated the numerical milestones within series by publishing books of particular merit. Name:

   *a.* Penguin No. 3000
   *b.* Penguin No. 4000
   *c.* Pelican No. 1000

*Publisher's Note*
THE FIFTIETH PENGUIN ANNIVERSARY

The competition closes on 31 March 1986. It is not open to staff of Penguin Books Ltd, their families or friends. The first prize is £100 worth of Penguin Books of your choice, and there are two runner-up prizes of £50 worth of Penguin Books apiece.

   Please send your answers to:

Dept BC
Penguin Books Ltd
536 King's Road
London SW10 0UH

# Part Two

??????????????????????????????

# The Answers

# Food and Drink

1. This was Evelyn Waugh writing in 1959 in the Preface to the new edition of *Brideshead Revisited* (1945). It is interesting to note that the undeniable *embarras de richesse* that Waugh found somewhat distasteful by this time contributed more than a little to its huge television success of the eighties. Possibly people actually *identified*?

2. This, of course, is old Sam. Johnson at his most elegiac and dogmatic, in 1779, according to Boswell's *Life*. One is tempted to wonder how he might have revised the breakdown were he living today. Malt whisky for heroes, possibly? And what would mere *men* drink? As for boys – they seem to alternate between cocktails full of vegetables and inhaling Evo-Stik, according to taste. (And for the record – then, as now – women do not drink.)

   The youth yearning a draught of vintage is John Keats forty years on in 'Ode to a Nightingale', as I am sure everyone knew. It's very sensual, this (he goes on to talk of his 'purple-stained mouth', as you will recall), but the famous line 'with beaded bubbles winking at the brim' has raised a few eyebrows in its time: why on earth should Keats have yearned for sparkling claret? Maybe it hadn't improved since Johnson was a lad.

3. This is Emma's opinion of Mr Elton in Jane Austen's *Emma* (1815). She finds herself alone in a carriage with him, with Mr Elton 'actually making violent love to her'. This, it transpires, consists of the taking of her hand, and speaking of his feelings for her; this makes one reflect on a few things: the ele-

gance and restraint of a more leisured era, of course. But I am also prompted to wonder at what vocabulary might have been left to re-create more spectacular happenings, had novelists of the time seen fit to do so. I am going to stop right now – I can sense the seething of Jane-ites everywhere.

The novel *Mr Weston's Good Wine* was published in 1927 – an allegorical work by T. F. Powys (1875–1953) in which Mr Weston ('God') sold his vintages ('Love and Death') from the back of a van. A modern classic, these days.

4. If you know both the Bible and Shakespeare backwards, this quiz question cannot have been much fun. But for those backing *some* knowledge with their flair for guessing, one or two surprises might emerge:

   a. The Bible. Ephesians 5:18
   b. The Bible. Ecclesiastes 9:7
   c. Shakespeare. *Othello*
   d. The odd man out, but it will have caught few of you. This, of course, is from Edward Fitzgerald's *The Rubáiyát of Omar Khayyám* (1859).
   e. The Bible. The Song of Solomon 7:9
   f. The Bible (Apocrypha). Ecclesiasticus 31:27
   g. Shakespeare. *King Lear*. The whole line deserves a mention: 'Wine loved I deeply, dice dearly, and in women out-paramoured the Turk.'
   h. The Bible. I Timothy 5:23. Every drunk's let-out.
   i. The Bible. Proverbs 20:1

5. a. J. P. Donleavy, 1955
   b. Shelagh Delaney, 1959

   *c.* Laurence Sterne, 1760–67 (nine volumes)

   *d.* This is the genuine wine book. Written by Evelyn Waugh, and published by Saccone & Speed, the wine merchant, in 1947, with decorations by Rex Whistler. A slim book, but a collector's item now, of course, and at the time of writing worth up to about a hundred pounds.

   *e.* W. Somerset Maugham, 1930

   *f.* P. G. Wodehouse, 1940. Who else could have got away with a title like that?

   *g.* J. P. Donleavy, 1971. Again.

   *h.* William Boyd, 1983

   *i.* Arnold Wesker, 1959 – also the author of that *other* non-foody work, *Chips With Everything* (1962).

**6.** Well yes, I agree – despite the clue, it might have been written by almost anyone. What I was trying to (half) get across was that it was in fact by the doyenne of food writers, Elizabeth David, in her quaintly titled *An Omelette and a Glass of Wine* – which, I admit, sounds a perfectly loathsome combination to me too, but I am *not* about to take on Ms David.

**7.** Indeed – neither is right. And it's not Johnson, either – or Orwell in satiric vein. Henry Fielding (1707–54) is the man in his little-known *The Grub Street Opera* (III, iii).

**8.** *a.* Although it *could* have been Dickens's Sam Weller, it was in fact R. S. Surtees in *Mr Jorrocks in Paris* – one of a highly entertaining series of sporting sketches which appeared in the 1830s and 1840s. Indeed, they have been seen as a forerunner to *The Pickwick Papers*.

b. Not really about champagne, I suppose – more about class and Englishness, in which contexts champagne always contrives to raise its lovely *mousse*. Anyway, it's Hilaire Belloc (1870–1953) in *On a Great Election*.

c. The sommelier is guiding Mr James Bond in Ian Fleming's first novel, *Casino Royale* (1953). The first of many, many bottles to be cracked as the Bond saga unfolded into the sixties. These Taittingers are one of the few things about the book to have dated – both would be undrinkable now – or have turned to near-sillery. (This is a nudge to those who have not yet solved the rider to this series of questions to persevere.)

d. This is a throwback to question 1 in this quiz, and is an example of Charles Ryder newly under the spell of Sebastian Flyte at Oxford. *Brideshead Revisited*, then; Evelyn Waugh, 1945.

e. The tongue-in-cheek comes from Tom Stoppard in *Travesties* (1975) – an extraordinary play which takes as its starter the fact that Lenin, Joyce and the Dadaist Tristan Tzara were all living in Zurich during the Great War.

And now the postscript. Sillery – a still white wine produced in the Champagne area of France – was the name given by Anthony Powell to the Oxford tutor quite reasonably chronicled by 'Nick Jenkins' in *A Dance to the Music of Time*. Maybe not as famous as Widmerpool (*no one* could put dear Kenneth Widmerpool in the shade), but notable for all that.

9. For a long time, people rather uncharitably assumed that it was Queen Victoria, but most now agree upon Queen Marie-Antoinette (1755–93). Although it is *attributed* to her, though (being French as she was, she is actually reputed to have said, 'Qu'ils mangent de la brioche'), there are records of very similar things having been said in France up to a hundred years earlier. It is possible that the Queen came across the idea in Rousseau's *Confessions* (1740) and stored away the *bon mot* until told that the poor had no bread, and then unleashed it with zeal. But whether knowing callousness, ignorance or a genuine unworldly and 'aristocratic' oblivion was behind the remark, I really could not say.

10. The first speaker is Jeeves, in *Stiff Upper Lip, Jeeves* (P. G. Wodehouse, 1963), at his most authoritative and blindingly *knowledgeable*. And the rather long-winded gastronome is Mr Bond again – this little lot was accompanied by the Taittinger in the champagne question. *Casino Royale* (Ian Fleming, 1953) – but 007 became more tolerable in later books.

# Quick-Fire Quiz

### Nineteenth-Century Works

1. R. M. Ballantyne, 1857
2. R. L. Stevenson, 1883
3. Jules Verne, 1873
4. Walter Scott, 1816
5. William Makepeace Thackeray, 1852
6. George Gissing, 1892
7. Charles Dickens, 1842
8. Anthony Trollope, 1873

9. W. W. Jacobs, 1896
10. Henry James, 1888
11. Emile Zola, 1885
12. George Eliot, 1861
13. Charles Kingsley, 1866
14. Rudyard Kipling, 1890
15. Bernard Shaw, 1893
16. R. L. Stevenson, 1889
17. Oscar Wilde, 1891
18. Mrs Gaskell, 1863
19. Nathaniel Hawthorne, 1851
20. Thomas Hardy, 1892 (revised 1897)

A fairly straightforward lot, though I suppose that numbers 6, 17 and 18 might have been a little troublesome. One hopes so, anyway.

## Quotation Titles

1. Thomas Hardy, 1874. From 'Elegy Written in a Country Churchyard' (1751), by Thomas Gray.

2. Agatha Christie, 1962. From 'The Lady of Shalott' (1833), by Tennyson.

3. These two books (by Dorothy L. Sayers, 1935,
& and Thom Gunn, 1961, respectively) derive
4. their titles from the same speech in Shakespeare's *Antony and Cleopatra*:

> Let's have one other gaudy night: call to me
> All my sad captains; fill our bowls once more;
> Let's mock the midnight bell.

5. W. Somerset Maugham, 1930. From Shakespeare again – *Twelfth Night*: 'Dost

thou think because thou art virtuous, there shall be no more cakes and ale?'

6. Ernest Hemingway, 1940. From 'Meditation XVII', by John Donne (1571?–1631): 'No man is an island . . . and therefore never send to know for whom the *bell* tolls; it tolls for *thee*.'

7. Noël Coward, 1941. From Shelley's 'Ode to a Skylark' (1819):

> Hail to thee, blithe spirit!
>     Bird thou never wert,
> That from heaven, or near it,
>     Pourest thy full heart
> In profuse strains of unpremeditated art.

8. H. E. Bates, 1958. From the great and famous Shakespeare sonnet: 'Shall I compare thee to a summer's day?'

9. Aldous Huxley, 1954. From William Blake's 'A Memorable Fancy': 'If the doors of perception were cleansed everything would appear as it is, infinite.'

10. P. D. James, 1962. From John Webster's *The Duchess of Malfi* (1623). Ferdinand says: 'Cover her face; mine eyes dazzle: she died young.'

11. Rosamund Lehmann, 1927. From George Meredith's *Modern Love* (1862):

> Ah, what a dusty answer gets the soul
> When hot for certainties in this our life!

12. John Berryman, 1970. From John Keats's 'When I Have Fears':

> Then on the shore
> Of the wide world I stand alone, and think
> Till love and fame to nothingness sink.

**13.** Ray Bradbury, 1953. From W. B. Yeats's 'The Song of Wandering Aengus':

> And pluck till time and times are done
> The silver apples of the moon
> And golden apples of the sun.

**14.** Thornton Wilder, 1948. From the Soothsayer's warning in Shakespeare's *Julius Caesar*: 'Beware the Ides of March.'

**15.** John Steinbeck, 1937. From Robert Burns's 'To a Mouse':

> The best laid schemes o' mice an' men
> Gang aft a-gley.

**16.** Sir Walter Scott, 1816. From Sir Thomas Browne's *Urn Burial* (1658): 'Old mortality, the ruins of forgotten times.'

**17.** Aldous Huxley, 1932. From Shakespeare's *The Tempest*:

> How many goodly creatures are there here!
> How beauteous mankind is! O brave new world,
> That has such people in't.

**18.** Vita Sackville-West, 1931. From John Milton's *Samson Agonistes* (1671):

> His servants he with new acquist
> Of true experience from this great event
> With peace and consolation hath dismiss'd
> And calm of mind all passion spent.

**19.** Graham Greene, 1940. From the Bible, St Matthew 6:9: 'For thine is the kingdom, and the power, and the glory, for ever, amen.'

**20.** Scott Fitzgerald, 1934. From John Keats's 'Ode to a Nightingale':

> Away! away! for I will fly to thee,
> Not charioted by Bacchus and his pards,
> But on the viewless wings of Poesy,
> Though the dull brain perplexes and retards:
> Already with thee! tender is the night,
> And haply the Queen-Moon is on her throne,
> Clustered around by all her starry Fays

---

# The Things Men (and Women) Do

1. Ebenezer Scrooge, *A Christmas Carol*, Charles Dickens, 1843
2. Billy Fisher, *Billy Liar*, Keith Waterhouse, 1963
3. Charles Ryder, *Brideshead Revisited*, Evelyn Waugh, 1945
4. Bathsheba Everdene, *Far from the Madding Crowd*, Thomas Hardy, 1874
5. Jane Eyre, *Jane Eyre*, Charlotte Brontë, 1847
6. Joe Lampton, *Room at the Top*, John Braine, 1957
7. Pinkie, *Brighton Rock*, Graham Greene, 1938
8. Silas Marner, *Silas Marner*, George Eliot, 1861
9. Arthur Seaton, *Saturday Night and Sunday Morning*, Alan Sillitoe, 1958
10. Jimmy Porter, *Look Back in Anger*, John Osborne, 1957
11. Hardcastle, *She Stoops to Conquer*, Oliver Goldsmith, 1773
12. Frederick Clegg, *The Collector*, John Fowles, 1963
13. Aziz, *A Passage to India*, E. M. Forster, 1924
14. Jim Hawkins, *Treasure Island*, R. L. Stevenson, 1883

15. Jim, *Empire of the Sun*, J. G. Ballard, 1984
16. Bilbo Baggins, *The Hobbit*, J. R. R. Tolkien, 1937
17. Falstaff, *The Merry Wives of Windsor*, William Shakespeare, 1623 (first folio)
18. Ernst Blofeld, *On Her Majesty's Secret Service*, Ian Fleming, 1963
19. Peter Pan, *Peter Pan*, J. M. Barrie, 1904
20. Raskolnikov, *Crime and Punishment* – no, just horsing around. In fact it was Bertie Wooster, *The Code of the Woosters*, P. G. Wodehouse, 1938.

---

# Quick-Fire Quiz

## Who Wrote (Twentieth Century)?

1. Lawrence Durrell (novel), 1935
2. Brian W. Aldiss (novel), 1955
3. P. G. Wodehouse (novel), 1902
4. Kingsley Amis (verse), 1947
5. V. S. Naipaul (novel), 1957
6. A. N. Wilson (novel), 1977
7. Beryl Bainbridge (novel), 1967
8. Graham Greene (verse), 1925
9. Samuel Beckett (verse), 1930
10. William Trevor (novel), 1958
11. Saul Bellow (novel), 1944
12. Graham Swift (novel), 1980
13. John Betjeman (verse), 1931
14. Tom Stoppard (novel), 1966
15. Malcolm Bradbury (novel), 1959
16. Muriel Spark (non-fiction), 1950
17. Anthony Burgess (novel), 1956
18. Salman Rushdie (novel), 1975

**19.** Margaret Drabble (novel), 1963
**20.** Mervyn Peake (juvenile), 1939

Some very well known, but quite a few surprises, I think. Numbers 1, 10, 12, 16 and 20 were probably the trickiest, so anyone who got fifteen right is probably grinning already.

# Children's Books

1. Although 'The Inklings' rather sounds as if it might be a minor work by J. R. R. Tolkien, it is not a book at all, but the name given to a group of literary friends in Oxford from 1930 and onwards. Tolkien was indeed one of its members, though its star was C. S. Lewis (author of the Narnia chronicles). Humphrey Carpenter (who has written a book about the circle entitled, simply, *The Inklings*) tells us that it was largely due to Lewis's encouragement that Tolkien's *The Lord of the Rings* trilogy was ever completed.

2. Mr Wilkins – whose Christian name, we discover somewhere along the line, is Lancelot – is the grumpy and often explosive master in the *Jennings* books, by Anthony Buckeridge, and he is played off against the more serene and philosophical Mr Carter. There were over twenty books about *Jennings* and Darbishire and Linbury Court School in the fifties and sixties, together with all the secondary lights – of whom Chas. Lumley ('Home Made Cakes and Bicycles Repaired') springs to mind. The books enjoyed an enormous success in their time, and despite (or maybe because of) their

intrinsic Englishness, they have been translated into about a dozen foreign languages from Welsh to Hebrew. In Germany, Jennings is known as Fredy, in France as Bennett, and in Norway he glories in the appellation Stompa.

3. *a.* Charlie, of Chocolate Factory fame (1972)
   *b.* James (1961)
   *c.* Danny (1975)
   *d.* George (1981)
   *e.* Mr Fox (1970)
   *f.* Willie Wonka (*Charlie and the Chocolate Factory*, 1964)

   The original *Chitty-Chitty-Bang-Bang* trilogy was written by Ian Fleming (1964–5) – his only venture into children's writing.

4. Right – here we go then. These are in order, but if you got all twenty-three, I shan't quibble about placing. In fact, if you got all twenty-three, one sincerely feels for you.

   1. *The Tale of Peter Rabbit*
   2. *The Tale of Squirrel Nutkin*
   3. *The Tailor of Gloucester*
   4. *The Tale of Benjamin Bunny*
   5. *The Tale of Two Bad Mice*
   6. *The Tale of Mrs Tiggy-Winkle*
   7. *The Tale of Jeremy Fisher*
   8. *The Tale of Tom Kitten*
   9. *The Tale of Jemima Puddleduck*
   10. *The Tale of the Flopsy Bunnies*
   11. *The Tale of Mrs Tittlemouse*
   12. *The Tale of Timmy Tiptoes*
   13. *The Tale of Johnny Town-Mouse*
   14. *The Tale of Mr Tod*
   15. *The Tale of Pigling Bland*
   16. *The Tale of Samuel Whiskers*
   17. *The Tale of the Pie and the Patty Pan*

18. *The Tale of Ginger and Pickles*
19. *The Tale of Little Pig Robinson*
20. *The Story of a Fierce Bad Rabbit*
21. *The Story of Miss Moppet*
22. *Appley-Dapply's Nursery Rhymes*
23. *Cecily Parsley's Nursery Rhymes*

5. A little bit annoying, wasn't it?

    a. Louisa M. Alcott, 1868
    b. Frances Hodgson Burnett, 1886
    c. Graham Greene, 1946
    d. Helen Bannerman, 1899
    e. Antoine de Saint-Exupéry, 1943 (English edition, 1945)
    f. Charles Perrault (first *credited* version, 1697)
    g. J. M. Barrie, 1902 (the forerunner of *Peter Pan in Kensington Gardens*)
    h. Alison Uttley (the character first appeared in 1929 in *The Squirrel, the Hare, and the Little Grey Rabbit*)
    i. Louisa M. Alcott, 1871
    j. Hans Christian Andersen, 1836

6. a. *The Wind in the Willows*, Kenneth Grahame, 1908
    b. *Stalky & Co.*, Rudyard Kipling, 1899
    c. *The Lion, the Witch, and the Wardrobe*, C. S. Lewis, 1950
    d. *Winnie-the-Pooh*, A. A. Milne, 1926
    e. *The Old Man of Lochnagar*, HRH The Prince of Wales, 1980
    f. *The Jungle Book*, Rudyard Kipling, 1894
    g. *Just William*, Richmal Crompton, 1922
    h. *Meet My Folks!*, Ted Hughes, 1961
    i. *The Water Babies*, Charles Kingsley, 1863
    j. *The Secret Garden*, Frances Hodgson Burnett, 1911

7. *a.* Charles Lutwidge Dodgson (1832–98)
   *b.* . . . *and What Alice Found There*; and . . . :
   *An Agony in Eight Fits.*
   *c.* An interesting tale. Of the 2,000 copies printed by Macmillan in 1865, only twenty presentation copies had been sent out when Carroll recalled them (he received eighteen of the twenty) when the illustrator Tenniel made it known that he was very displeased with the quality of the printing of the plates. This entire initial printing was considered quite good enough for America, however, and was sold to the New York publisher Appleton in bound and unbound sheets, and these were mostly sold in the USA in 1866 as the first American edition. The *second* (and superior) printing was sold late in 1865 in Britain as the *first* edition, though dated 1866 on the verso of the title page. Thus the *true* first edition was printed by Macmillan in 1865, and sold in America the following year, while the *official* first edition was also printed (later) in 1865, sold in 1865, but dated 1866. The 'Appleton' edition could fetch £15,000 and up today, while the *official* first edition (which is in fact a reprint) might be worth £1,000–2,000.
   *d.* Mervyn Peake.
   *e.* *i.* The Dodo
      *ii.* The March Hare
      *iii.* The Duchess
      *iv.* Alice herself – as Carroll tells us: 'she was so much surprised she quite forgot how to speak good English.'
      *v.* The King to the White Rabbit

8. The *Dandy* is the oldest, born in 1937, and the *Beano* followed on a year later. They are still

the best-selling comics in Britain, as are the Christmas annuals which these days tend to appear in July, and vanish before autumn. *Noddy* is a comparative youngster – the first book, *Noddy Goes to Toyland*, appeared in 1949. It occurs to me that I haven't mentioned in either the question or the answer that he was created by Enid Blyton.

# Quick-Fire Quiz

### Fictitious Characters

1. *Kenilworth*, Walter Scott, 1821
2. *Look Back in Anger*, John Osborne, 1957
3. *Brighton Rock*, Graham Greene, 1938
4. *Bleak House*, Charles Dickens, 1852–3
5. *Room at the Top*, John Braine, 1957
6. *Wuthering Heights*, Emily Brontë, 1847
7. *The Wind in the Willows*, Kenneth Grahame, 1908
8. *Brideshead Revisited*, Evelyn Waugh, 1945
9. *The Diary of a Nobody*, George and Weedon Grossmith, 1892
10. A choice: *Cakes and Ale*, Somerset Maugham, 1930, or *Cider With Rosie*, Laurie Lee, 1959
11. *Three Men in a Boat*, Jerome K. Jerome, 1897
12. *Far from the Madding Crowd*, Thomas Hardy, 1874
13. *The Merchant of Venice*, William Shakespeare, 1596 (this is the date when it is believed that the play was written)
14. *A Passage to India*, E. M. Forster, 1924
15. *The Flight from the Enchanter*, Iris Murdoch, 1956
16. *Ulysses*, James Joyce, 1922 (1st *book*)
17. *Robinson Crusoe*, Daniel Defoe, 1719

18. *The Tale of Johnny Town-Mouse*, Beatrix Potter, 1918
19. *Jake's Thing*, Kingsley Amis, 1978
20. *Waiting for Godot*, Samuel Beckett, 1952

A mixed bunch, as far as difficulty goes. I think that numbers 1, 8 (Aloysius was Sebastian's teddy, by the way) and 15 might have caused a bit of trouble. And number 20 too, but no one is going to admit it.

## Quick-Fire Quiz

### Sleuth

1. Ernest Bramah
2. R. Austin Freeman
3. G. K. Chesterton
4. Edgar Wallace
5. Margery Allingham
6. Ngaio Marsh
7. John Dickson Carr
8. S. S. Van Dine
9. Rex Stout
10. Nicholas Freeling
11. John Creasey (as J. J. Marric)
12. Michael Innes (J. I. M. Stewart)
13. Nicholas Blake (C. Day-Lewis)
14. Wilkie Collins (in *The Moonstone*)
15. Herbert Jenkins
16. Freeman Wilis Crosts
17. H. R. F. Keating
18. A. E. W. Mason
19. Dorothy L. Sayers (rather conveniently, he married Lord Peter Wimsey's sister)
20. Arthur Conan Doyle (Baynes, of the Surrey Constabulary, was the only policeman who ever won Holmes's respect)

# Crossword

| | | | | | | | | | | | | | | | |
|---|---|---|---|---|---|---|---|---|---|---|---|---|---|---|---|
| ¹T | O | ²M | | ³B | U | ⁴S | T | | ⁵B | ⁶A | R | ⁷B | E | ⁸R |
| A | | A | | O | | H | | | | N | | A | | I |
| ⁹T | H | R | A | C | I | A | N | | ¹⁰E | G | G | C | U | P |
| L | | T | | C | | K | | | | E | | O | | |
| ¹¹E | R | I | C | A | | ¹²E | ¹³A | S | T | L | Y | N | N | ¹⁴E |
| R | | N | | C | | S | T | | | I | | | | D |
| | | | | ¹⁵C | O | P | P | E | R | P | ¹⁶L | A | T | E |
| ¹⁷E | | ¹⁸A | | I | | E | V | | E | | N | | | N |
| ¹⁹R | E | S | T | O | R | A | T | I | O | N | | | | |
| I | | H | | | R | | E | | D | | ²⁰B | | ²¹A | |
| ²²C | H | E | A | ²³P | N | E | S | S | | ²⁴E | V | A | N | S |
| | | N | | E | | | M | | | N | | R | | I |
| ²⁵I | N | D | I | A | N | | ²⁶L | I | O | N | I | S | E | D |
| N | | E | | K | | | T | | | I | | E | | E |
| ²⁷K | E | N | N | E | R | | ²⁸W | H | O | S | | ²⁹T | A | S |

## Scored Lead-On Quiz

1. *a.* We always refer to her as *Fanny Hill.*
   *b.* It was written by John Cleland, and published in 1748–9. It brought him twenty guineas, he was summoned before the Privy Council on a charge of indecency (discharged) and the publisher enjoyed a vast sale and made £10,000. Truly, the profits of porn were most unequal shared. Today, at least, *everybody* makes a bomb.

2. *a.* The elegant and splendid Stephen Potter, in 1947.
   *b.* *Notes on Lifemanship* (1950), *One-Upmanship* (1952), *Supermanship* (1958). A perfectly amiable film was made, based upon all four books (*School for Scoundrels,* 1960), which offered not only Ian Carmichael and Terry-Thomas, but the sublime Alastair Sim, as Potter himself.

3. *a.* Margaret Mitchell, in 1936.
   *b.* Interesting to know what people might have come up with. The truth is, that following this bestselling and Pulitzer-Prize-winning first novel, and following the sensation of the film (1939), Margaret Mitchell wrote nothing else whatever: that rare bird, who drives publishers wild. She is on record as saying that she simply did not believe herself to be a good writer, and few, it must be said, have queued up to contradict her. Maybe she just didn't *give* a damn.

4. *a.* Christopher Marlowe, 1604
   *b.* William Combe is the man who wrote this book (1812) together with several sequels.

They all concern this somewhat preposterous clergyman, but are best known now for the marvellous Rowlandson cartoons that accompanied them ('Dr Syntax with the Bookseller' I find particularly amusing).

5. *a.* Charlotte Brontë, *Jane Eyre*, 1847. So famous, this line, as to have nearly become a parody of the genre. But a startling approach to the denouement, for all that.
   *b.* Much less well known: Jane Austen, *Persuasion*, 1818. Prior to the discovery that the butler did it, people at the ends of books tended to get married.

6. *a.* Wackford Squeers was the villain of the piece, with his noisome son, to whom he had extended the patronym.
   *b.* Henry Samuel Quelch – he of the gimlet eye, a rather painful affliction, I always thought.

7. *a.* Easy. Raymond Chandler.
   *b.* Just as easy, really: Dashiell Hammett. Here's looking at you, kid.

8. *a.* It's extraordinary how very recent knowledge can slip away: Anita Brookner, *Hotel du Lac*, and . . .
   *b.* . . . *Life and Times of Michael K*, by one J. M. Coetzee.

9. *a.* T. S. Eliot – in his very first published work, *Prufrock and Other Observations* (1917).
   *b.* Ezra Pound, 1920

10. *a.* Jerome K. Jerome (*ça va sans dire*) and then J. (J.K.J. himself), Harris (Carl Hentschel) and George (George Wingrave).

    *b.* Montmorency – he who pined to contribute a water rat to Harris's stew, and damn near got his way.

SCORING

| | |
|---|---|
| 30 points | You must be seen to be brilliant, and also unbearable. And not altogether trustworthy. |
| 25–29 | A superb performance! Any lucky guesses? |
| 20–24 | Your knowledge is very sound – sound enough for you to be enjoying yourself. |
| 15–19 | Still very very good. I mean it. |
| 10–14 | Yes, well – I daresay you *would* have done better had you spent longer on it. Or maybe you thought the phrasing of the questions ambiguous? Anyway, you weren't really in the mood – touch of a headache – and scoring quizzes is anyway very silly. Isn't it. |
| 0–9 | You don't really like this book very much, do you? |

## Famous Last Words

1. According to T. S. Eliot, 'the first, the longest and the best of modern detective novels' – *The Moonstone*, Wilkie Collins, 1868. (These last words of the novel are followed by an epilogue.)
2. John Fowles, *The Magus*. This is from the original 1966 version; the ending in the 1977 revised edition – though substantially the same – differs in quite a few ways.

3. Siegfried Sassoon, *Memoirs of a Fox-Hunting Man*, 1928
4. Charles Dickens, *David Copperfield*, 1849–50
5. Emily Brontë, *Wuthering Heights*, 1847
6. Laurence Sterne, *The Life and Opinions of Tristram Shandy*, nine volumes, 1759–67
7. George Orwell, *Animal Farm*, 1945
8. Thomas Hardy, *Jude the Obscure*, 1896
9. Kingsley Amis, *Lucky Jim*, 1953
10. James Joyce, *Ulysses*, 1922

## Acrostic

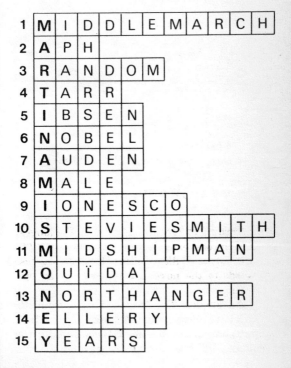

```
1   M I D D L E M A R C H
2   A P H
3   R A N D O M
4   T A R R
5   I B S E N
6   N O B E L
7   A U D E N
8   M A L E
9   I O N E S C O
10  S T E V I E S M I T H
11  M I D S H I P M A N
12  O U Ï D A
13  N O R T H A N G E R
14  E L L E R Y
15  Y E A R S
```

## Quick-Fire Quiz

### Semi-Titles

1. ... *Barset* (Anthony Trollope, 1867)
2. ... *Rainbow* (Virginia Woolf, 1958)
3. ... *Evans?* (Agatha Christie, 1934)
4. ... *Wildfell Hall* (Anne Brontë, 1848)
5. ... *Chickens* (P. G. Wodehouse, 1906)
6. ... *Damned* (F. Scott Fitzgerald, 1922)
7. ... *'The Narcissus'* (Joseph Conrad, 1897)
8. ... *Gilbert Pinfold* (Evelyn Waugh, 1957)
   ... *Richard Feverel* (George Meredith, 1859)
9. ... *Baronet* (Wyndham Lewis, 1932)
10. ... *Spy* (John le Carré, 1974)
11. ... *Midlothian* (Walter Scott, 1818)
    ... *The Matter* (Graham Greene, 1948)
12. ... *Innocent* (Alexander Solzhenitsyn, 1969)
13. ... *Mori* (Muriel Spark, 1959)
14. ... *, 20* (Kingsley Amis, 1971)
15. ... *Summer* (Aldous Huxley, 1939)
16. ... *the Pickwick Club* (Charles Dickens, 1836–7)
17. ... *the Whole* (Baron Corvo, 1934)
18. ... *Elephant* (George Orwell, 1950)
19. ... *a Lady* (Henry James, 1881)
20. ... *Dorian Gray* (Oscar Wilde, 1890)

## Call My Bluff

Well, of course if your vast knowledge and reading extended to your recognizing the words right away, there is not much hope for either of us, one way and another. Otherwise, you will want the solutions. How perceptive are you? How gullible are you? How good a liar am I? When am I going to get on with it?

1. *b.* I shouldn't think it's used much any more,
though. I rather liked the public school
slang, myself – it would be good to hear
people drawling, 'Oh, don't talk such
Armenian bole!' I myself shall start today.
2. *c.* Sometimes in life, the boring is true. Quite
often, actually.
3. *c.* A bit of a gamble, this one – I think a lot of
people might have known the rather
amusing *How to Avoid Matrimony* and,
when you fail, *How to Survive Matrimony*.
They could easily be updated and reissued,
were not Waterhouse currently engaged in
a thousand other things.
4. *a.* And do not feel too badly about never having *heard* of her best-known work *The
Gates Ajar*.
5. *c.* The Dürer bit was meant to make you
smell a rat – the inclusion of the only
German artist the man has ever heard of.
But no – no rat: all of it is true.
6. *a.* All the classicists will have swooped on
this one – but the Pound possibility might
have given them pause. I myself would
have plumped (we had to have a plump) for
the *Doctor's Dilemma* nonsense, which
says more about me than words ever can.
7. *b.* Although not a name you encounter in
Spain much these days.
8. *a.* Yes, Martha it is – but if there was any
poetry left in the world, it would be the
bookseller, Jules.
9. *b.* And rather amusing it is too.
10. *c.* Dickens strikes again. The James Bond
stew sounded enticing, though, didn't it?

I have just noticed that none of the *d*s were the
correct answer; I could not at present put my
finger on the reason, but I feel convinced that this
is in all probability Freudian.

## You've Read the Book, Now Answer Questions about the Film!

1. *Jane Eyre* (Charlotte Brontë)
2. *Brighton Rock* (Graham Greene)
3. *Look Back in Anger* (John Osborne)
4. *Goldfinger* (Ian Fleming)
5. *Pride and Prejudice* (Jane Austen)
6. *The Maltese Falcon* (Dashiell Hammett)
7. *Gone with the Wind* (Margaret Mitchell)
8. *Oliver Twist* (Charles Dickens)
9. *The Great Gatsby* (Scott Fitzgerald)
10. *Wuthering Heights* (Emily Brontë)

11. David Storey, 1960. Richard Harris
12. John Osborne, 1957. Laurence Olivier
13. Alan Sillitoe, 1958. Albert Finney
14. Alan Sillitoe, 1959. Tom Courtenay
15. John Braine, 1957. Laurence Harvey
16. Shelagh Delaney, 1959. Rita Tushingham
17. Iris Murdoch, 1961. Richard Attenborough
18. Jack Trevor Story, 1963. Ian Hendry
19. Lynne Reid Banks, 1960. Leslie Caron
20. Stan Barstow, 1960. Alan Bates

# Quick-Fire Quiz

## Authors' First Books

1. *Sketches by Boz* (1836–7)
2. *The Macdermots of Ballycloran* (1847)
3. *Desperate Remedies* (1871)
4. *An Inland Voyage* (1878)
5. *The Lay of the Last Minstrel* (1805)
6. *On the Stage – and Off* (1885)
7. *Scenes of Clerical Life* (1858)
8. *Almayer's Folly* (1895)
9. *Workers in the Dawn* (1880)
10. *Antonina* (1850)
11. *Sartre: Romantic Rationalist* (1953)
12. *A Painter of Our Time* (1958)
13. *Encounters: Stories* (1923)
14. *Shadow Dance* (1966)
15. *This Side of Paradise* (1920)
16. *Where Angels Fear to Tread* (1905)
17. *Night Fears, and Other Stories* (1924)
18. *Chamber Music* (1907)
19. *The White Peacock* (1911)
20. *Afternoon Men* (1931)

# Crossword

| 1 B | 2 A | 3 R | 4 R | I | E | | 5 T | H | E | 6 W | A | 7 V | E | 8 S |
|---|---|---|---|---|---|---|---|---|---|---|---|---|---|---|
| | R | | I | | N | | H | | | H | | I | | T |
| | A | 9 P | A | T | E | R | | 10 M | E | R | C | E | R | |
| | B | C | E | | E | | | E | | T | | | | A |
| 11 R | E | C | O | U | R | S | E | 12 A | L | T | O | | | C |
| | L | R | | T | | M | | E | | E | | R | | H |
| | L | 13 D | I | A | M | E | T | 14 E | R | | I | | | E |
| 15 O | A | R | S | | I | | N | | V | | 17 L | A | 18 D | Y |
| L | 16 O | | 19 A | N | T | I | G | O | N | E | | | E | |
| I | U | | N | | N | | C | | G | | | | A | |
| P | 20 S | T | O | P | | 21 A | D | A | M | B | E | D | E | |
| H | S | | U | | | B | | T | | R | | | B | |
| 22 A | M | E | L | I | A | | 23 O | V | I | N | E | | E | |
| N | | A | | L | | | A | | O | | A | | A | |
| 24 T | O | U | G | H | E | S | T | | 25 N | I | K | I | T | A |

## Acrostic

| | | | | | | | | | |
|---|---|---|---|---|---|---|---|---|---|
| 1 | J | A | M | E | S | | | | |
| 2 | A | R | A | M | I | S | | | |
| 3 | N | A | B | O | K | O | V | | |
| 4 | E | V | E | L | Y | N | | | |
| 5 | A | R | N | O | L | D | | | |
| 6 | U | T | O | P | I | A | | | |
| 7 | S | P | E | N | D | E | R | | |
| 8 | T | H | O | R | N | E | | | |
| 9 | E | D | W | I | N | D | R | O | O | D |
| 10 | N | I | G | H | T | A | N | D | D | A | Y |
| 11 | E | N | D | G | A | M | E | | | |
| 12 | M | A | R | L | O | W | E | | | |
| 13 | M | U | T | L | A | R | | | | |
| 14 | A | G | A | T | H | A | | | | |

## Sex

Torrid stuff, wasn't it? Well, all is serene now for we have reached the climax. There follows the naked truth:

1. This was the good Doctor Johnson in conversation with the actor David Garrick, in 1750, as reported by Boswell in his *Life*.

**2.** Humbert Humbert trembling on the brink of his nymphet: Vladimir Nabokov's *Lolita* (1959). Do you remember the opening? 'Lolita, light of my life, fire of my loins. My sin, my soul. Lo-lee-ta: the tip of the tongue taking a trip of three steps down the palate to tap, at three, on the teeth. Lo. Lee. Ta.'

**3.** Geoffrey Chaucer, the scamp. It is the Wyf of Bath talking in the sixth of *The Canterbury Tales*.

**4.** Sigmund Freud at his most provocatively Freudian. From the essay 'Transformations of Puberty' of 1905, contained in the volume *Three Essays on Sexuality*.

**5.** One of the greats: James Joyce's *Ulysses* (1922).

**6.** Oh, what larks! Philip Larkin's opening stanza of '*Annus Mirabilis*' contained in the volume *High Windows* (1974).

**7.** This is the appalling, smug and imaginative Frank Harris in his 1,000-page *My Life and Loves*. Bilge, of course; this was one of the milder encounters of hundreds. No woman could resist him, and we have his word on it.

**8.** Subtler than most limericks, I think. Anthony Burgess in *Earthly Powers* (1980).

**9.** This *had* to be written by a woman, and a sensualist at that: Colette, *The Ripening Seed*, 1923 (English edition, 1949).

**10.** The man without whom no quiz of this nature would seem complete: D. H. Lawrence, *Women in Love*, 1921.

# Quick-Fire Quiz

## Poetical Terminology

1. Unrhymed iambic pentameters, with a ten-syllable line.
2. Two vowel sounds pronounced as one.
3. A break where a word ends, before a foot is finished.
4. Two successive lines of verse that rhyme.
5. Poem, originally intended to be sung, addressed to someone, or something.
6. A five-line jingle, rhyming AABBA. Example (anonymous):

> There once was a couple named Mound
> Whose sexual control was profound;
> When engaged in coition,
> They had the ambition
> To study the *Cantos* by Pound.

7. Japanese lyric of seventeen syllables split into three lines of five, seven, and five.
8. Poem of fourteen lines.
9. The fourteen lines split into three groups of four, and followed by a couplet, rhyming ABAB CDCD EFEF GG.
10. The fourteen lines split into two groups of eight and six; the eight-line group must rhyme ABBAABBA, while the six-line group may be looser.
11. Free-form verse, relying heavily upon its visual impact on the printed page. It can be split

> up
> in any way for
> no particular
> rea
>
>                 son.

12. A pair of rhymed couplets rhyming AABB – usually about someone. E. Clerihew Bentley was the eponymous deviser, and he contributes this example:

> It was a pity about Dickens'
> Insane jealousy of chickens,
> And one could really almost weep
> At his morbid mistrust of sheep.

13. A continuous narrative poem, celebrating a hero or an event.

In the following answers, a long syllable is signified ´ and a short syllable is signified ˘.

14. Iambus: ( ˘ ´ )
15. Anapest: ( ˘ ˘ ´ )
16. Dactyl: ( ´ ˘ ˘ )
17. Spondee: ( ´ ´ )
18. Pyrhhic: ( ˘ ˘ )
19. Tribrach: ( ˘ ˘ ˘ )
20. Trossachs: A woodland glen between lochs Katrine and Achray in Perthshire, Scotland. I do not know what this is doing here either; I can only imagine that we were both thinking of trochees ( ´ ˘ )

# Quick-Fire Quiz

## Pseudonyms

Confusing business. And Bertie Wooster was nearly caught up in it all in P. G. Wodehouse's story *Bingo and the Little Woman*: 'Bingo had told him that I was the author of a lot of mushy novels by Rosie M. Banks, you know. Said that I had written them, and that Rosie's name on the title-page was my what d'you call it.'

1. Charles Hamilton
2. William Sydney Porter
3. René Raymond
4. Henry Vincent Yorke
5. David Cornwell
6. D. J. Watkins-Pitchford
7. Harry Summerfield Hoff
8. Frederick Rolfe
9. Gertrude Stein
10. Karen Blixen
11. Hector Hugh Munro
12. H. C. McNeile
13. Kenneth Millar
14. Arthur Wade
15. Brian O'Nolan
16. Leslie Charles Bowyer Yin
17. Robert Bruce Montgomery
18. John Beynon Harris
19. Émile Herzog
20. John Anthony Burgess Wilson

# The 'Double-Devilish' Bookagram

| 1 M<br>I | 2 H<br>H | 3 I<br>E | 4 L<br>A | 5 J<br>R | 6 C<br>D | | 7 G<br>T | 8 I<br>H | 9 K<br>E | | 10 I<br>F |
|---|---|---|---|---|---|---|---|---|---|---|---|
| 11 C<br>I | 12 K<br>R | 13 I<br>S | 14 J<br>T | | 15 H<br>R | 16 E<br>U | 17 M<br>M | 18 E<br>O | 19 G<br>U | 20 I<br>R | 21 B<br>I |
| 22 D<br>N | | 23 L<br>T | 24 A<br>H | 25 I<br>E | | 26 K<br>M | 27 O<br>I | 28<br>D | 29<br>D | 30 I<br>L | 31 N<br>E |
| 32 N<br>O | 33 M<br>F | | 34 H<br>A | 35 J<br>N | | 36 B<br>A | 37 M<br>R | 38 O<br>G | 39 C<br>U | 40 M<br>M | 41 L<br>E | 42 O<br>N |
| 43 B<br>T | | 44 F<br>W | 45 J<br>I | 46 C<br>T | 47 N<br>H | | 48 O<br>M | 49 G<br>Y | | 50 G<br>B | 51 E<br>R | 52 F<br>O |
| 53 D<br>T | 54 O<br>H | 55 G<br>E | 56 N<br>R | | 57 L<br>W | 58 O<br>H | 59 G<br>E | 60 B<br>N | | 61 K<br>I | | 62 N<br>W |
| 63 A<br>A | 64 O<br>S | | 65 A<br>T | 66 F<br>R | 67 K<br>Y | 68 O<br>I | 69 A<br>N | 70 N<br>G | | 71 N<br>T | 72 C<br>O |
| 73 B<br>P | 74 N<br>E | 75 L<br>R | 76 F<br>S | 77 J<br>U | 78 G<br>A | 79 E<br>D | 80 F<br>E | | 81 F<br>H | 82 E<br>I | 83 B<br>M |
| 84 K<br>N | 85 M<br>O | 86 K<br>T | | 87 I<br>T | 88 M<br>O | | 89 J<br>M | 90 O<br>A | 91 M<br>R | 92 C<br>R | 93 A<br>Y |
| 94 C<br>B | 95 M<br>U | 96 J<br>T | | 97 A<br>I | 98 G<br>T | | 99 N<br>D | 100 B<br>I | 101 H<br>D | | 102 E<br>N | 103 K<br>O |
| 104 H<br>T | | 105 A<br>S | 106 C<br>E | 107 F<br>E | 108 M<br>M | | 109 B<br>M | 110 F<br>U | 111 A<br>C | 112 G<br>H | | 113 M<br>M |
| 114 B<br>O | 115 D<br>R | 116 J<br>E | | 117 A<br>T | 118 D<br>H | 119 I<br>A | 120 E<br>N | | 121 I<br>A | | 122 F<br>D | 123 I<br>I |
| 124 C<br>S | 125 E<br>T | 126 O<br>R | 127 E<br>A | 128 B<br>C | 129 O<br>T | 130 A<br>I | 131 F<br>O | 132 J<br>N | | | |

| | 111 | 24 | 37 | 97 | 105 | 65 | 123 | 63 | 69 | 130 | 117 | 93 |
|---|---|---|---|---|---|---|---|---|---|---|---|---|
| A | C | H | R | I | S | T | I | A | N | I | T | Y |

| | 73 | 36 | 60 | 43 | 114 | 83 | 100 | 109 | 21 | 128 | | |
|---|---|---|---|---|---|---|---|---|---|---|---|---|
| B | P | A | N | T | O | M | I | M | I | C | | |

| | 124 | 39 | 94 | 106 | 6 | 11 | 46 | 72 | 92 | |
|---|---|---|---|---|---|---|---|---|---|---|
| C | S | U | B | E | D | I | T | O | R | |

| | 22 | 85 | 115 | 53 | 118 |
|---|---|---|---|---|---|
| D | N | O | R | T | H |

| | 18 | 51 | 79 | 82 | 120 | 127 | 102 | 125 |
|---|---|---|---|---|---|---|---|---|
| E | O | R | D | I | N | A | N | T |

| | 44 | 52 | 122 | 80 | 81 | 131 | 110 | 76 | 107 |
|---|---|---|---|---|---|---|---|---|---|
| F | W | O | D | E | H | O | U | S | E |

| | 7 | 112 | 59 | 50 | 55 | 78 | 19 | 98 | 49 |
|---|---|---|---|---|---|---|---|---|---|
| G | T | H | E | B | E | A | U | T | Y |

| | 2 | 34 | 66 | 101 | 15 | 16 | 104 |
|---|---|---|---|---|---|---|---|
| H | H | A | R | D | R | U | T |

| | 3 | 121 | 13 | 87 | 25 | 20 | 8 | 119 | 30 | 10 |
|---|---|---|---|---|---|---|---|---|---|---|
| I | E | A | S | T | E | R | H | A | L | F |

| | 35 | 77 | 14 | 5 | 45 | 89 | 116 | 132 | 96 |
|---|---|---|---|---|---|---|---|---|---|
| J | N | U | T | R | I | M | E | N | T |

| | 9 | 84 | 103 | 12 | 26 | 61 | 86 | 67 |
|---|---|---|---|---|---|---|---|---|
| K | E | N | O | R | M | I | T | Y |

| | 57 | 4 | 23 | 41 | 75 |
|---|---|---|---|---|---|
| L | W | A | T | E | R |

| | 17 | 95 | 108 | 113 | 1 | 33 | 88 | 91 | 40 |
|---|---|---|---|---|---|---|---|---|---|
| M | M | U | M | M | I | F | O | R | M |

| | 31 | 99 | 70 | 74 | 62 | 32 | 56 | 71 | 47 |
|---|---|---|---|---|---|---|---|---|---|
| N | E | D | G | E | W | O | R | T | H |

| | 42 | 27 | 38 | 54 | 129 | 48 | 90 | 126 | 68 | 64 | 58 |
|---|---|---|---|---|---|---|---|---|---|---|---|
| O | N | I | G | H | T | M | A | R | I | S | H |

## Scored Lead-On Quiz

1. *a.* Collins, under whose 'Crime Club' imprint, Christie became undisputed queen.
   *b.* Chapman & Hall – the firm's early success being very largely due to Charles Dickens. By the time of Evelyn Waugh's first novel, *Decline and Fall*, his father Arthur was chairman and managing director of the firm. Nepotism only played a role as to Evelyn designing his own dust-wrapper, for the novel was and is indisputably magnificent.

2. *a.* Kingsley Amis, for his James Bond novel *Colonel Sun. Not* a spoof, but an excellent evocation – *far* better than subsequent attempts from other hands.
   *b.* Cyril Connolly, for his classic *The Unquiet Grave*. The first edition was published by his own 'little magazine' *Horizon* (1,000 copies only).

3. *a.* Robert Graves, 1934. The sequel was *Claudius the God*.
   *b.* This was the autobiography of that rather elegant journalist Claud Cockburn, whose surname, I once told an American, was pronounced like the port; to this day he calls him Clod Harvey.

4. *a.* If one didn't know, one might have known: George Bernard Shaw stirring it up in *Dramatic Essays and Opinions* (1907).
   *b.* According to Boswell, Johnson averred this in 1769. But Johnson's esteem for Shakespeare was very high – as, indeed, was that of Shaw.

**5.** *a.* Virginia Woolf, 1933

   *b.* If one knows the answer to this, the question seems trite and its solution unremarkable; otherwise, it is rather bizarre. It is the biography of Elizabeth Barratt Browning's dog and not, it must be said, one of Virginia Woolf's monuments.

**6.** *a.* Dick Francis, 1957

   *b.* Notable for the fact that it was his autobiography. Since then, Francis has published increasingly successful crime novels (with a turf connection) and has made himself one of Britain's best-selling writers.

**7.** *a.* André Maurois

   *b.* One did not want to give away *too* much detail, here, but it was the first *English* paperback that caused the stir; and it has to be admitted that the book itself had little to do with the kerfuffle. In 1935, Allen Lane selected it to be Penguin No. 1 in his launch list of ten. Blue-banded (code: biography), dust-wrappered, and priced at 6d – 2½ pence, to you.

**8.** *a.* *Dracula*, Bram Stoker

   *b.* *Frankenstein*, Mary Wollstonecraft Shelley

**9.** *a.* John Berger, 1972

   *b.* Thomas Pynchon, 1963

**10.** *a.* These personages comprised the entire contents of Lytton Strachey's *Eminent Victorians* (1918).

   *b.* Lytton Strachey again – some of the people he dealt with in *Books and Characters* (1922).

SCORING

Just thinking about it, I rather think that the full thirty points *was* a possibility with this quiz (this said to just slightly deflate those select few of you who honestly attained them). That said, you would really have to know your stuff, or else have taken *ages* over the thing, or else (horrors) used reference! This is unforgivable; it's *compilers* who do that. I should think half-marks (fifteen) about average here, so anyone with twenty up has cause for glee. If you got less than ten – don't tell a soul, or blame it on your maths.

## Acrostic

```
 1  T  H  U  R  S  D  A  Y
 2  H  A  P  P  Y
 3  O  L  I  V  E  R
 4  M  A  I  A
 5  G  E  O  R  G  E
 6  U  P  W  A  R  D
 7  N  U  N  N  E  R  Y
 8  N  E  W  C  O  M  E  S
 9  M  O  R  R  I  S
10  O  R  T  O  N
11  L  O  V  E
12  Y  E  A  T  S
```

# Records

1. Frank Richards is the man, apparently – real name Charles Hamilton, 1875–1961. He created old Bunter, of course, but when the *Gem* and the *Magnet* were the most popular boys' papers in the country, Richards was writing every word of both, every week, as well as other odds and ends, such as novels, in his spare time. One *has* heard talk that other hands ghosted for him and, on the basis of the figures to follow, it does seem possible: an average of 80,000 words a *week* (a typical novel of today might run to only 60,000) and a total of 100 million words (give or take one or two) during his lifetime. This works out at about two hundred *War and Peace*s, though, it must be said, with infinitely more laughs.

2. Frederick Forsyth, if we are to believe the hype – and it is less painful not to: a total of three million pounds for *The Fourth Protocol*, before the book was published. Doesn't it make you think? Or something?

3. Miss Cartland. Christie has sold only about three hundred million copies, in over a hundred languages, while young Barbara – although translated into a mere seventeen languages – has notched up three hundred *and seventy* million copies (and more, by the time I get this typed). A truly extraordinary lady (as she *will* keep on reminding us) who has published nearly 400 titles – in 1977, 1980 and 1981 publishing twenty-four books *in each year*; I expect she was just gripped by that age-old authorial need to *say* something.

4. No, Christie doesn't quite make it: Erle Stanley Gardner pips her at the time of writing. He has sold about twenty million more than Agatha Christie's 300 million. This figure, incidentally (this is an attempt to instil a sense of proportion into a highly disproportionate area) is about five times the population of the British Isles.

5. Laurence Eusden (1688–1730) is the undersung Laureate, while William Wordsworth was the 73-year-old, assuming office in 1843, and dying seven years after. The longest-*lived* Laureate, by the way, was John Masefield, who died in 1967 at the age of nearly eighty-nine, while the poet who held the chair for the longest period of time was Tennyson – nearly forty-two years.

6. $2,400,000 in 1978 (then, equivalent to about half as many pounds) for one of only twenty-one known complete copies of Gutenberg's Bible, printed in Mainz, Germany, in 1454 – the first printed book. By way of comparison, a First Folio of Shakespeare (1623) was sold at auction in 1985 for $638,000 (about half a million pounds) which strikes me as a bargain.

7. Well, although there was a South African lady named Kathleen Lindsay who apparently published 904 of the things, the names one is more likely to recognize are Ursula Bloom, with about 520 to her credit, and John Creasey who, under his many pseudonyms, published no less than 560. (There is also some nonsense abroad about his having received over 750 rejection slips before his first novel was accepted, but I shouldn't think even the current *Writers' and Artists' Yearbook*

runs to that many publishers, even inter-
nationally, so the figure is probably apoc-
ryphal. There is little evidence anyway that
an unpublished writer could have the *heart* to
submit a book that many times, this due to
many things apart from the frailty of the
spirit; there spring to mind the elusiveness of
immortality, and the price of stamps.)

8. Not so straightforward, wouldn't you know it.
As long ago as 1978, the Oxford University
Press were celebrating a quincentenary – but
they admitted that this anniversary marked
five hundred years of printing in Oxford,
rather than under the banner of the Press,
ancient though it is. The *Cambridge* University Press, however, has been printing and
publishing constantly since 1584, and therefore, at just over 400 years, it qualifies as the
oldest.

9. Penguin Books – *not* for *The Book Quiz Book*, I
am distressed to relate – but for the first
*unexpurgated* edition of D. H. Lawrence's
*Lady Chatterley's Lover*, following the historic
trial. They printed three million copies in
1960, and the book was on sale everywhere –
alongside evening newspapers, in sweet-
shops, everywhere. For many hundreds of
thousands it must have been the first Penguin
to have entered their home, and one must
relish their disappointment in discovering a
complicated and resonant work of creative
fiction in place of whatever they might have
been led to expect – and for three-and-six too!
Penguin sales now approach five million.

10. *Ulysses*? No, nothing like that: brace
yourselves. I am appalled to tell that the
twentieth-century bestseller is none other

than Jacqueline Susann's *Valley of the Dolls*, first published in 1966, and to date enjoying a worldwide sale of 28–30 million copies. Thank God this is the last question in this particular quiz. [*Yes, enough records. Ed.*]

# The 'Midas' Quiz

1. Kenneth Grahame, 1895
2. Margaret Drabble, 1967
3. Joseph Heller, 1979
4. Apuleius. We don't quite know when the thing was written, or very much about the man. He was born around AD 125, and lived to be (about) fifty.
5. Penelope Fitzgerald, 1977
6. P. G. Wodehouse, 1904
7. J. G. Frazer, twelve volumes, 1890–1915
8. Henry James, 1904
9. Doris Lessing, 1962
10. Margaret Drabble, 1975
11. ... of *Best Songs and Lyrical Poems in the English Language* by F. T. Palgrave, 1861.
12. John Steinbeck, 1929
13. James Stephens, 1912
14. Ian Fleming, 1965. The man who wrote *Goldfinger*.

# Crossword

|   | C | H | R | I | S | T | I | E |   | P | U | C | K |   |
|---|---|---|---|---|---|---|---|---|---|---|---|---|---|---|
| S |   | O |   | N |   | H |   | L |   | A |   | H |   | T |
| C | O | R | O | N | E | R |   | M | A | S | S | E | U | R |
| O |   | N |   | I |   | E |   |   | T |   | E |   |   | O |
| T | O | U | T | S |   | E | M |   | M | A | R | V | E | L |
|   |   | N |   | F |   | S |   | M |   |   | E |   |   | L |
| T | U | G |   | R | O | C | H | E | S | T | E | R |   | O |
| O |   |   |   | E |   | O |   | M |   | H |   |   |   | P |
| R |   | C | H | E | E | R | Y | B | L | E |   | R | U | E |
| E |   | E |   | E |   | E |   | E |   | S |   | E |   |   |
| A | N | D | T | E | N |   | U | R |   | A | U | D | E | N |
| D |   | I |   | L |   |   | S |   | U |   | C |   |   | O |
| O | B | L | I | G | E | D |   | H | A | R | L | O | W | E |
| R |   | L |   | I |   | I |   | I |   | U |   | A |   | L |
|   | C | A | I | N |   | O | P | P | O | S | I | T | E |   |

## Clichés

Thought it had to be a pushover because they all had to be Shakespeare, did you? Well, the schemes of mice and men . . .

1. John Milton, *Paradise Lost*, 1667
2. Jonathan Swift, *My Lady's Lamentation*, 1728
3. Dante's *Inferno* – finished just before his death in 1321. Being Italian, he actually wrote: *Lasciate ogni speranza voi ch'entrate!*
4. 'Accidents will occur in the best regulated families' runs the full quotation – Mr Micawber in Dickens's *David Copperfield*, 1849–50.
5. The *first* recorded use is very probably not the best known:

   > The valiant Knight of Triermain
   > Rung forth his challenge-blast again,
   > But answer came there none

   This is Walter Scott in *The Bridal of Triermain* (1813). It was used again by Lewis Carroll in *Through the Looking-Glass* (1871):

   > But answer came there none –
   > And this was scarcely odd because
   > They'd eaten every one.

6. The best known of all: Mr Bumble in Dickens's *Oliver Twist* (1837–8). He further avers that the law is also 'a idiot'.
7. Apparently the first time that writing was ever referred to as 'black and white': the authority of print. Ben Jonson, *Every Man out of His Humour*, 1599.
8. James Hervey, *Reflections on a Flower-Garden*, 1746. The quotation runs:

   > E'en crosses from his sov'reign hand
   > Are blessings in disguise.

9. This was number 16 of *The Dolly Dialogues* by Anthony Hope (1894).
10. None other than Aristophanes, who lived from *c.*444 BC to *c.*380 BC. The extraordinary word (in its closest rendition from Greek to English) comes up in *Birds*, as a suggestion for the name of the capital city of birds.
11. Yes, Shakespeare: *A Midsummer Night's Dream*.
12. Alexander Pope, *An Essay on Criticism*, 1711
13. Shakespeare again. This is Lady Macbeth talking, but the deed turns out to be not *quite* done; as Macbeth says, 'We have scotch'd the snake, not killed it.'
14. Rudyard Kipling, from (what else?) 'The Ballad of East and West'.
15. Kipling again, from (what else?) 'The Female of the Species'.
16. This is Tennyson, from *In Memoriam* (1850), though the idea could have stemmed from Arthur Hugh Clough's 'Peschiera', where the same couplet appears, save the word 'loved' which is replaced by 'fought'. Cynics would tell you that they are much of a muchness.
17. Archimedes (287–212 BC) came up with this little gem. It translates, rather pathetically, as 'I've got it!'
18. The Bard, of course: *Twelfth Night*.
19. The Bible, Timothy 6:10.
20. The rather underrated Ian Hay in his play *The Housemaster*, of 1936.

## Book Collecting

1. *a.* Simply an author in whom collectors are currently interested; this usually means the quest for that author's first editions.

All *great* writers are collected, I think, but there are a number of very good writers who, for one strange reason or another, have never excited the interest of collectors. And yes, it must be admitted too that one or two (or three) highly collectable authors are really rather mediocre. Further than this I will not say.

b. No, they do not mean the same. A 'collected set' means that the bookseller has assembled a group of books (again, usually in first edition) by the one collected author – although the word 'set' should not be taken to mean that *all* the author's books are present. A 'collected edition' comprises those books put out by publishers in uniform bindings and dust-wrappers (that is, on the rare occasions when they do not decide to change the entire concept halfway through) when their authors have achieved inalienable eminence – and, *ergo*, sales. By definition, these are reprints, and should not command very high prices – but if the edition is *complete*, or if the author's work is currently not in print (and hence not otherwise available) this need not at all be the case.

2. This truly does reflect the vagaries of book collecting, and I offer these figures without comment:

   a. £15,000
   b. £2,000
   c. £300
   d. £10,000
   e. £2,000,000
   f. £5
   g. £1,000
   h. £15,000

  *i.* £150
  *j.* £800
  *k.* £100
  *l.* £250

**3.** *a.* Modern is generally now taken to mean twentieth century, although works of the 1880s and 1890s by such as Hardy, Wells, Doyle and Yeats may also be included. The 1920s to 1960s is the largest area, but nothing can be *too* modern: a book by a collected author published this morning is fine.

    *b.* This term continues to shift as the supply of *truly* early books dries up completely. *Incunabula* (books printed in the fifteenth century) used to be synonymous with 'early', and then the rather loose 'post-*incunabula*' was coined instead. This does not mean just *anything* post – of course not – but anything *just* past. 'Early printed' today means anything printed up to about 1650; thus, a Shakespeare First Folio (1623) or anything by, say, Donne are completely OK, while first editions of even such as Richardson or Fielding or Defoe would not qualify. (Jolly nice to have, all the same, though.)

**4.** *a.* Dust-wrapper (the bit of paper around the book)

    *b.* Title-page (the page that announces the title and author)

    *c.* Endpaper (the fixed and loose pages attached to the boards)

    *d.* Out of print

    *e.* Very good condition

    *f.* All edges gilded (as opposed to TEG, which stands for simply *top* edge gilded)

    *g.* With all faults. This sometimes follows a

price that is known to be on the low side for the book in question, and denotes the fact that the bookseller is aware of the copy's shortcomings, and that these are reflected in the price.

*h*. Nothing to do with the *Times Literary Supplement*. This refers to a Typed Letter, Signed – as opposed to ALS which denotes an *autograph* (i.e. handwritten) letter, signed.

5. *a*. What *is* one to say about the eponymous Thomas Bowdler? He was a Scottish doctor who, in 1818, published *The Family Shakespeare*. This, he vouchsafed, was an edition suitable for the whole family – even women – from which all 'profanity and indecency' had been cut. And heavily cut too. *Romeo and Juliet*, *Antony and Cleopatra* and *King Lear* are particularly severely dealt with, while of *Othello* Bowdler simply despaired; he thought it 'unfortunately little suited for family reading' and recommended that it be kept well out of harm's way. And this preposterous edition of the Bard was laughed off the face of the earth, right? No, not at all. It went through very many editions, keeping Bowdler comfortable while he attacked Gibbon's *Decline and Fall of the Roman Empire* with similar gusto, and a true doctor's zeal for incision (not to say wholehearted amputation).

*b*. James Granger (1723–76) pre-dated Bowdler, and could not have had a more different outlook. He published his *Biographical History of England* in 1769, and left many blank leaves interspersed in the text so that purchasers could add illustrations of their choice at will. Thus, a 'Grangerized' book is an extra-illustrated one, and the hobby became rather fashionable at the time, among people with nothing better to do.

6. This term is reserved for mid-nineteenth-century novels which were published in three matching volumes. This was quite the common practice (such as Hardy's *Tess of the D'Urbervilles* was published in this way), the reasoning behind it being that, as most people *borrowed* fiction from private lending libraries at a shilling a time (this is five pence, for the benefit of the kids, and a hell of a lot of hundred years ago), the novels would circulate rather faster (and hence more profitably) if the borrower had to return for successive volumes. Only the *very* rich actually bought novels, for these three-deckers were traditionally priced at half-a-guinea *per volume* – astounding when you consider that an entire novel might have been purchased for that a century on. It even makes the ten and twelve pound novels of today look almost cheap. Almost.

7. *a.* This means that the folded sheets that make up a signature (sewn section) have not been slit open by the binder's guillotine, or the purchaser's knife. Collectors have long been lambasted for preferring books in this (unreadable) state, but, as any collector knows, having books one cannot possibly read liberates oases of time which can be spent acquiring more.

   *b.* This does not mean the same thing at all: a more complicated business altogether. The term 'uncut' is universally (and wrongly)

used to describe the above state (unopened), but nor does it refer to the rough
fore-edges that are left *after* opening; nor
yet does it mean the state of having been so
published – with the fore-edge left shaggy
and not smoothly cut prior to deckling or
gilding.

What it *does* mean is that the large
margins around the printed text have not
been hewn to nothing by a succession of
binders; the rough edges, therefore, are not
cherished *per se*, but as evidence that the
pages (and so the book) are of original size.

8. Although the earliest *printed* dust-wrapper is
about 150 years old (1832, to be exact), there is
evidence that *plain* paper was wrapped
around books by booksellers for quite some
while earlier than that, as the forerunner of
the paper bag. By no means all books since
1832 were issued with a dust-wrapper, however; indeed, for the ensuing decades it
seemed the exception rather than the rule,
and a dust-wrapper earlier than the mid-
1880s is extremely rare today. As the twentieth century progressed, of course, a
dust-wrapper became mandatory, and its
sophistication and glossiness increased in in-
verse proportion to the attention bestowed
upon the case, which now has succumbed to
the starkly utilitarian. It was the Modern
First Edition collecting boom of the 1920s that
really brought the dust-wrapper to the fore,
and the boom of the 1980s has bestowed even
more importance upon the presence of a clean
example – so much so that unless a book is
very rare indeed it is very hard to place an
unwrapped copy unless it is stupidly cheap
– and sometimes even then. In some cases
today, the dust-wrapper can account for 75 per

cent of the value of the book. Aren't you relieved that this is a paperback, and you don't have to worry?

If you are interested in knowing more about this sort of thing, I commend to you Joseph Connolly's *Modern First Editions: Their Value to Collectors* (Orbis, 1984). Objectively speaking, it's wonderful.

9. *a.* A. A. Milne, illustrated by E. H. Shepard.
  *b.* Lewis Carroll, illustrated by John Tenniel.
  *c.* J. R. R. Tolkien, and illustrated by the author.
  *d.* Richmal Crompton, illustrated by Thomas Henry.
  *e.* Arthur Conan Doyle, illustrated by Sidney Paget.
  *f.* Roald Dahl, illustrated by Quentin Blake.
  *g.* T. S. Eliot, illustrated by Nicholas Bentley (this was the 1940 edition – the *first* edition (1939) was unillustrated, but bore a dust-wrapper by Eliot himself).
  *h.* Kenneth Grahame, illustrated by E. H. Shepard.
  *i.* John Lennon, with his own inimitable drawings.
  *j.* Alison Uttley, illustrated by Marie Tempest.

10. *a.* The function dictates the form. These are the binder's ropes that keep the sewn sections together.
  *b.* A full binding is one where the entire book is hand-bound in leather or, less usually, buckram or vellum. A half-binding is where only the spine and corners are covered with the material, the boards being paper, sometimes marbled; and a quarter-binding has a covered spine only.

c. A strange idea, this, but rather effective. During the course of binding, the fore-edge of the printed and clamped pages is slightly fanned out, whereupon a painting – often a landscape – is executed, the surface being the edges of every page. The book is then allowed to resume its customary form, and then the edge is gilded in the normal way – thus, the painting is only revealed when the book's pages are once more fanned out, and at all other times is protected from dust by the gilding.

d. Gilding is a three-fold business, as hinted at above. Firstly, it keeps out the light from the pages and plates, thus reducing the likelihood of foxing (those brownish liver spots); secondly, it keeps the dust out (mainly the top edge for this) and hence reduces dirt and discoloration; and thirdly, it looks wonderful. The top edge is seen to be the minimum necessary, but as gilding is carried out in real gold leaf, it is a rather expensive (as well as painstaking) business; *three* gilded edges, therefore, tend to be reserved for the more opulent bindings.

e. Not really a binding at all, this, but a box that contrives to look like one. Invented by Daniel Charles Solander (1736–82), originally to store botanical specimens, the potential for ephemera, pamphlets or rare and flimsy material was soon realized. It is a sort of a box-file, then, which – because of a binder's attention to the spine – is indistinguishable from a book when on the shelf.

# True or False?

1. Yes, quite true. Not remotely surprising in Christie or Wodehouse, I should have thought – they just pushed off and beavered away – but Simenon (who has written more than the other two put together) has been very busy in other ways – chiefly the acquisition of carnal knowledge of *thousands* of women, this aided and abetted by cognac and pipe tobacco. And *he's* the one who's still alive.

2. Yes, true. The man's two *middle* names, however, were Josef Konrad. He was born of Polish parents, but he Anglicized his name when he decided to devote his life to writing in English – his third language.

3. No, not by two hundred years. Dante was born in 1265, about *three* hundred years before Shakespeare.

4. Well, it might have been, of course, but we never learn whether or not Fagin has a first name at all, so False. (Maybe he started out with a first name, and sold it.)

5. No she isn't. A. S. Byatt is, though.

6. No, this is a quotation from Fitzgerald's *Rubáiyát of Omar Khayyám*. The 'Sans Eyes, Sans Teeth . . .' one is *As You Like It*.

7. This is true, but it was far from Chaucer's original intention. In the Prologue we learn that each of the *twenty-nine* pilgrims is to tell four stories each – a total of 116!

8. This is about as false as false can be – the Runcible Cat is Edward Lear, not Eliot.

9. What utter rot. No, it was to be Penguin from the first.

10. Yes, true, he did. Isn't it *delicious*?

11. No, it isn't. Nothing to do with the shaking bit: when he *had* a vodka-martini, that's how he liked it. But he had very few, and all this

Dom Perignon '55 is nonsense too – an invention of the films. Bourbon was Bond's drink, and lashings of it.

12. Yes, true – but the book was not turned down on *literary* grounds, it must be understood.

13. Yes, I am afraid this is so. The novel's unrelenting fatalism and tragedy were castigated by everybody. Hardy wrote only poetry for the rest of his life.

14. False, false, false. This is repeated in order to placate outraged Proustians and, more particularly, Frenchmen. No, it was Poirot who was the Belgian.

15. I made up every word. Sounds the sort of thing he *might* have said, though – doesn't it. Anyway: false.

16. No, it was never uttered at all. Once – and only once – Holmes vouchsafed to Watson that a problem was 'elementary', but that was it. Thus, the unquenchable power of legend.

17. Almost. It *was* printed in 1633, but it was written by John *Ford*.

18. Yes, true on both counts. This is easy to remember, as every household always has five of the six *Second World War*s, and three of the four of the other one. (No one, it must be added, seems much to *care* about this shortfall.)

19. False. He has only written one novel, but it was also his first published work: *The Rock Pool* (1936).

20. I regret to say that this is false. Too good to be true.

## Acrostic

| | | | | | | | | |
|---|---|---|---|---|---|---|---|---|
| 1 | E | V | E | R | D | E | N | E |
| 2 | M | I | L | T | O | N | | |
| 3 | I | R | I | S | | | | |
| 4 | L | O | V | I | N | G | | |
| 5 | E | N | D | L | E | S | S | |
| 6 | Z | O | O | | | | | |
| 7 | O | U | T | O | F | P | R | I | N | T |
| 8 | L | A | O | D | I | C | E | A | N |
| 9 | A | L | I | C | I | A | E | |
| 10 | N | E | W | | | | | |
| 11 | A | U | T | H | O | R | | |
| 12 | N | A | N | C | Y | | | |
| 13 | A | R | A | M | I | S | | |

## Scored Lead-On Quiz

1. *a.* Giacomo Casanova, of course. His extraordinary *Mémoires* (twelve volumes,
1826–38) were a true (??) account of all his
close encounters of the carnal kind – *twelve*
volumes, you will have digested. It is interesting to note in passing that although
Casanova had already published a number
of historical works in his native language,
Italian, for his *Mémoires* he rejected the
more romantic tongue in favour of the
earthier French.

*b.* Don Juan was not a romancer, and his
name is now a byword for the heartless and
sometimes even cruel seducer; still, at
least he was eventually delivered unto the
devils, who doubtless have limitless
experience in dealing with his sort.

He apparently did exist – Don Juan
Tonorio of Seville – and was first written
about in 1630 by Gabriel Tellez, who,
under the pseudonym 'Tirso da Molino',
wrote a play entitled *El burlador de Sevilla*
(the jester, or deceiver, of Seville). The
subject has seemed to be irresistible stuff
for the stage, for Don Juan has been the
centre of plays by Molière, Shadwell, Gol-
doni, Montherlant, Pushkin and Shaw
(*Man and Superman*), to say nothing of
Mozart's *Don Giovanni*.

But for the purposes of this quiz, I
suppose you can have your two points if
you came up with Byron's unfinished epic
satire of 1819–24.

2. *a.* The *Strand*, a magazine founded in 1891
by George Newnes. Conan Doyle had published many stories elsewhere – including
two Holmes adventures, which had not
made much of a splash – before contribu-
ting a series that came to be known as *The
Adventures of Sherlock Holmes*. The series
was very, very popular (the *Strand*'s read-
ership was 300,000) and Sidney Paget's
illustrations rendered them indelible. It is
very doubtful whether Holmes would have
been so instant and huge a success without
the *Strand*; and the *Strand*, certainly,
were very eager to retain Conan Doyle's
services, constantly beating off more
lucrative offers from rival and less well-
known magazines – by the simple and

proven device of paying even more. The magazine issued blue-bound volumes containing six months' issues, and although these precede the publication of Sherlock Holmes in book form, they have never commanded the high prices from collectors that you might expect – unlike the subsequent books, which fetch hundreds. The *Strand* magazine kept going until 1950, when it folded.

b. *A Study in Scarlet* was the first (*one* point for that) and it appeared in *Beeton's Christmas Annual* of 1887 (the twenty-eighth issue). This soft-covered volume could fetch up to £4,000 from collectors today – probably more in America, and certainly more in 1987, the Sherlock Holmes centenary.

3. a. John le Carré, published by Gollancz in 1960, and followed two years later by a similarly little-known title, *A Murder of Quality*. His first novel did introduce us to George Smiley, though, but le Carré published quite a lot of stuff before he saw fit to arrange his return in the *Tinker, Tailor* trilogy. His best-known book is still his third – *The Spy Who Came In from the Cold* (1963).

b. Frederick Forsyth is the man – a fact maybe known only to collectors. The book was a non-fiction account of the situation as it was then in Biafra, written by Forsyth in his journalistic capacity and published as a Penguin Special (paperback) in 1969. *The Day of the Jackal* came in 1971, and the rest is money-spinning history.

4. *a.* This is the great epistolatory novel by the undisputed master of the form, Samuel Richardson; indeed, the book is often regarded to be the genesis of the English novel. It was published in three volumes (1740–41) and entirely comprises fictional letters and journals, ingeniously interwoven to form a narrative. The drawbacks of such a vehicle are, of course, very soon obvious, and they were spotted with unseemly haste by . . .

   *b.* . . . Henry Fielding, who in the same year as the publication of *Pamela*'s third volume brought out (pseudonymously) *An Apology for the Life of Mrs Shamela Andrews* – the work later growing into the novel *Joseph Andrews*. Fielding had been irritated by what he saw as mawkish hypocrisy and sentiment on the part of Richardson (this referring to the *substance* of the book: Fielding might well have been irked also by its success) and in his travesty he transformed the virtuous Pamela into Shamela the trollop. Fielding's authorship was known, though never officially acknowledged, and Richardson very much took the satire to heart, and felt bitterly towards Fielding for the rest of his life, never forgiving him.

5. *a.* All were not only poets (I hope *no one* tried to get away with that one) but Poets Laureate.

   The very first Poet Laureate was Ben Jonson, although the title was not officially bestowed on him; James I conferred on him a pension in 1616. Apart from the poets named in the question, the other Laureates have been d'Avenant, Shad-

well, Tate, Eusden, Cibber, Whitehead,
Warton, Pye, Austin, Bridges, Masefield,
Day-Lewis and Betjeman. The present
incumbent is, of course, Ted Hughes.

b. Yes, playwrights, if you will – but *that* isn't
going to get you two points. All Nobel
Prizewinners for Literature, in 1934, 1936,
1969 and 1964, respectively. Sartre was
one of only two writers to have officially
declined the prize since its inauguration in
1901 (the other was Boris Pasternak, in
1958). Since 1901, the national writers of
France have won the most times (eleven),
though there have been eighteen winners
who write in the English language –
in order of receipt: Kipling, Tagore,
Yeats, Shaw, Sinclair Lewis, Galsworthy,
Eugene O'Neill, Pearl S. Buck, T. S. Eliot,
Faulkner, Churchill, Hemingway, Steinbeck, Beckett, Patrick White, Saul Bellow
and William Golding.

6. a. *Widowers' Houses* (1893). By this time,
Shaw had written – in addition to his jour-
nalism and music criticism – five novels,
which had achieved only a very moderate
success. Reading his frequently damning
(though ever immaculate) condemnations
of *other* people's plays at the time, one
sometimes feels that he was driven towards writing for the stage only in order to
ensure for himself a grand night out
whenever he chose to visit a theatre. But
he really did deliver; his plays remain
among the very finest we have.

b. This, in one sense, was a swine of a question, although it might also be seen as a
gift, for within certain limits one can be as
right or as wrong as one likes, if you see

what I mean. As usual with Shakespeare we are stymied by our ignorance of any solid, bedrock *fact*. Although his poetry was published during his lifetime – *Venus and Adonis*, *The Rape of Lucrece* and the *Sonnets* – none of his plays was *properly* printed until the First Folio of 1623, seven years after his death. (To make this clearer, it is understood that about half his plays were circulated in partial and unauthorized copies, as transcribed from the performances themselves – these now referred to as 'bad quartos'.) And so to readdress oneself to the question, one thinks that the three parts of *Henry IV* and *Richard III* were the earliest plays *written*, but that first publication can only be said to be within the First Folio of 1623. The printing of these commenced early the previous year, and about 1,200 copies were produced. These were sold at about £1 each (which I *know* seems a bargain, and you'll take ten – but it was a colossal sum over 350 years ago). A rather healthy 230 examples survive, and one was sold in 1985 for about half a million pounds. Inflation.

I charge you to award yourself the full two points only if you think you have said enough of all this to honestly deserve them.

7. *a.* The range of your reading and your special tastes will determine whether or not you have the answers to part *b* in this place, and vice versa. Anyway. All these novels were written by Agatha Christie, and published in 1942, 1962, 1961 and 1968, respectively.

b. Yes, all the titles are quotations – but did
   you know from *where*?

   *i.* 'The moving finger writes; and having
   writ, moves on' (Edward Fitzgerald,
   *The Rubáiyát of Omar Khayyám*,
   1959)

   *ii.* Out flew the web and floated wide,
   The mirror crack'd from side to side
   Tennyson, *The Lady of Shalott*, 1833

   *iii.* 'And I looked, and behold a pale horse:
   and his name that sat on him was
   death' (the Bible, Revelation 6:8)

   *iv.* By the pricking of my thumbs,
   Something wicked this way comes
   Shakespeare, Second Witch, *Macbeth*

**8.** *a.* C. K. Scott Moncrieff was the man, and
   Terence Kilmartin did the revision –
   which, does, I own, contrive to make the
   boring bits less so. The title, of course, is
   *Remembrance of Things Past*.

  *b.* From the top: *Swann's Way*, *Within a Bud-
   ding Grove*, *The Guermantes Way*, *Cities of
   the Plain*, *The Captive*, *The Fugitive* and
   *Time Regained*.

**9.** *a.* *Everyone* said Betjeman – and you are
   right. Take your point as you fondly
   remember him in his pork-pie hat
   and woolly, rhapsodizing over Ruislip
   Underground.

  *b.* Now there are *two* others, actually, and I
   imagine that your answer will tally with
   your age. The first – and he pre-empts
   Betjeman in its usage – is Evelyn Waugh,
   who wrote of one Margot Metroland in
   several of his novels, but most notably in
   his first, *Decline and Fall* (1928), where

she starts life as Margot Best-Chetwynde. The other author who *might* have come to mind is Julian Barnes (he of *Flaubert's Parrot*), whose first novel was entitled, simply, *Metroland*. Take your two points for either answer – but if you got *both*, give yourself a pat and have a smirk, in lieu of a bonus.

**10.** *a.* *The Rachel Papers* (1973), *Dead Babies* (1975), *Success* (1978), *Other People* (1981), *Money* (1984)

*b.* *Lucky Jim* (1953) – now it gets tougher – *That Uncertain Feeling* (1955), *I Like It Here* (1958), *Take a Girl Like You* (1960), *One Fat Englishman* (1963). Although this is only a ten-year span, interspersed among the above novels were three slim volumes of verse, a Fabian tract, a book of short stories and a study of science fiction.

SCORING

Anyone who scored thirty points, or somewhere near, is, shall we say, a phenomenon. *I* couldn't get the full thirty right now, and I've just written out all the answers. But I should think half-marks is average, in this quiz – if you got less than fifteen, you probably miscounted and did yourself out of five points somewhere along the line. Don't you think? Anything above this, though, is really very good, as it demonstrates that your knowledge goes deeper than the superficial facts. Indeed, I shall stick my neck out and say – I've started, so I'll finish – that any score over twenty is excellent.

# Quick-Fire Quiz

## Household 'Name' Reference Books

1. Architecture of the British Isles, in counties.
2. The legendary travel guides for every corner of the world, though foodies and others now swear by Michelin.
3. Pottery and porcelain.
4. *Modern English Usage*, of course. He still reigns supreme.
5. Well, you *could* get away with etymology – as in Johnson's Dictionary – but I think people today would more probably intend *Hugh* Johnson, and therefore wine.
6. *Phrase and Fable*.
7. Opera.
8. He of the famous *Thesaurus*: antonyms and synonyms.
9. The vast work on art and artists.
10. Words, loosely, but loose words in particular: slang.
11. Poems – the *Golden Treasury*.
12. The standard one-volume on the history of architecture.
13. Cricket.
13. *Trees and Shrubs*. Definitive.
15. Maybe it never *used* to be referred to as Harvey, but it certainly must now: *The Oxford Companion to English Literature*, prior to Margaret Drabble's 1985 update.
16. Art, with leanings to its psychology.
17. Aristocracy, and so on.
18. The huge dictionary of music.
19. World events of the past year.
20. Almost anything, really. Like why one should be driven to frittering time on quizzes, when one could be dreaming.

## Author Identification

I think there were no give-aways here – and the
damnable thing is that if you got *one*, by definition
you got *two* wrong. Slip up more than four times,
and you have a shambles on your hands. Anyway,
here we go:

1. – *d.* Lawrence Durrell, *Tunc*, 1968
2. – *g.* Ernest Hemingway, *Across the River and into the Trees*, 1950
3. – *k.* Ian Fleming, *Dr No*, 1958
4. – *i.* Iris Murdoch, *An Unofficial Rose*, 1962
5. – *m.* Len Deighton, *Billion Dollar Brain*, 1966
6. – *e.* Graham Greene, *It's a Battlefield*, 1934
7. – *n.* P. G. Wodehouse, *The Old Reliable*, 1951
8. – *b.* Dick Francis, *The Danger*, 1983
9. – *a.* D. H. Lawrence, *The Plumed Serpent*, 1926
10. – *o.* Frederick Forsyth, *The Dogs of War*, 1974
11. – *f.* Colin Wilson, *Necessary Doubt*, 1964
12. – *l.* C. P. Snow, *Last Things*, 1970
13. – *j.* Kingsley Amis, *Russian Hide and Seek*, 1980
14. – *c.* Norman Mailer, *The Deer Park*, 1957
15. – *h.* Muriel Spark, *The Only Problem*, 1984

## Odd One Out

1. Adrian Mitchell is the oddity here – the other
   three formed the band known as 'The Liverpool Poets', and their work was featured in
   such things as *The Mersey Sound* (1967) and

*The Liverpool Scene* (1967). Without doubt, the Penguin Modern Poets volume brought them to a national audience, but then Liverpool was very, dare I say, trendy at the time, this fuelled, I have my suspicions, by a pop group of the day named The Beatles.

2. You *could* argue that Shaw is the weirdness, on account of the others are poets, but it's a bit weak, isn't it? I mean – a bit *obvious*? Where can there be a more tenuous link? Well, what I was hoping for is that some of you might have come up with the truth that whereas Yeats, Shaw and Eliot are all Nobel prizewinners, Auden is not.

3. The first three are all related by blood (father and two daughters) whereas Strachey was related merely by inclination.

4. This one was just a question of knowledge, and sorting out all these weird and wonderful books without being deflected from one's initial assurance. *Jorrocks* is the oddity, as it was written by R. S. Surtees, while the remaining three are all by Tobias Smollett.

5. No, not the Folio Society because they give you slip-cases, and the others don't. Collins Crime Club is the odd man out, because – unlike the others – it is not a *club* at all (you don't join, you are not sent books, there is no subscription) but simply the name bestowed upon its illustrious crime list – the star of which is still Agatha Christie – by the publisher Collins. The others, as I say, are proper book clubs where more often than not you pays your money, and you takes their Choice. (*Pace*, Folio Society – I didn't mean it.)

6. Perfectly transparent, this one. George Bernard Shaw is the stranger, because throughout his career he had the temerity to use his real name, whereas the other 'Georges' conceal, in order, Amandine-Aurore Lucile Dupin (Baronne Dudevant), Mary Ann Evans and Eric Blair. In the case of the Baronne, you can see her point – 'George Sand' has a lot more snap to it.

7. The oddity in this rather odd quartet is *1983* for the simple reason that it is not a book title, and the others are – written by (respectively) Alasdair Gray, George Orwell and Anthony Burgess.

8. Stop torturing yourself, and stop thinking about India; nothing to do with India at all. Salman Rushdie, Ruth Prawer Jhabvala and J. G. Farrell have all won the Booker Prize, and Shiva Naipaul hasn't. (V. S. Naipaul has, however, and that's why I didn't choose him.)

9. Well – Mrs Gaskell, of course. A real flesh-and-blood person, and a writer to boot. All the others are characters in novels that bear their names – *The History of Mr Polly* by H. G. Wells, *Mr Norris Changes Trains* by Christopher Isherwood, and *Mrs Dalloway* by Virginia Woolf.

10. If you are a Greyfriars fan, you will have pounced on this one as being glaring, otherwise it might have caused a pause for thought. Nugent, Wharton and Hurree Jamset Ram Singh (the Nabob of Bhanipur, in case you need telling) are three of Frank Richards's Famous Five, the other two being Bull and Cherry. *Berry*, of course, is the character from a series of novels by Dornford Yates. The quizfulness is terrific.

# Quick-Fire Quiz

## Characters in Series

1. The CIA man in Ian Fleming's James Bond books.

2. The elegant young peer in the Remove at Greyfriars: the Bunter books, by Frank Richards.

3. The inimitable Kenneth Widmerpool from Anthony Powell's *A Dance to the Music of Time* sequence.

4. The handyman from Brian W. Aldiss's trilogy.

5. Head of skool, captain of games, also winner of mrs joyful prize for rafia work, ect. From the Nigel Molesworth quartet, by Geoffrey Willans and Ronald Searle.

6. If I had said the surname, all would have been revealed; he is Mycroft Holmes – Sherlock's brother. Conan Doyle.

7. Nothing to do with the old *Daily Mirror* comic strip – this is a *book* quiz. She is, of course, half the famous grunt: 'Me Tarzan – you Jane.' Edgar Rice Burroughs.

8. The ghastly little Bott child from Richmal Crompton's *William* books – the one who kept threatening to thqueam and thqueam.

9. One of the third form circle in Anthony Buckeridge's *Jennings* books, along with Darbishire, Atkinson, Temple and Bromwich Major.

10. One of the 'Co.' in Rudyard Kipling's *Stalky & Co.* stories.

11. The po-faced policeman in Enid Blyton's *Noddy* books – just to prove that she at least gave us a generic term.

12. The prize-winning pig at Blandings, and apple of the eye of P. G. Wodehouse's Lord Emsworth.

13. Guy Crouchback in Evelyn Waugh's *Sword of Honour* trilogy.
14. One of Biggles's companions in W. E. Johns's books.
15. One of Rupert's companions in stories begun by Mary Tourtel in 1920, and carried on by Alfred Bestall.
16. George Smiley, by John le Carré, notably from the *Tinker, Tailor* . . . trilogy, though he made his first appearance in le Carré's first book, *Call for the Dead*.
17. The narrator is C. P. Snow's *Strangers and Brothers* series.
18. The mastermind behind the magical car in Ian Fleming's trilogy *Chitty-Chitty-Bang-Bang*.
19. P. G. Wodehouse again, but this time the *Jeeves* stories. She is the one who invariably makes Bertie's life a misery and, according to him, chews broken bottles and wears barbed wire next to the skin.
20. The spy from Len Deighton's first three books – the Secret Dossiers – *but* we know his name only from the portrayal of the character in the films by Michael Caine. In the books, he is never named.

# Crossword

| | | | | | | | | | | |
|---|---|---|---|---|---|---|---|---|---|---|
| ¹L | ²I | ³T | ⁴E | ⁵R | A | T | U | R | ⁶E | ⬛ | ⁷D | ⬛ | ⁸T |

(grid)

Across/Down answers shown in grid:

- LITERATURE
- AROUSE
- TRAVESTY
- SCHILLER
- CLIO
- AMERICANS
- POLEMIC
- ONTARIO
- ACTONBELL
- AMIS
- ROYALIST
- ERIDANUS
- EVINCE
- MANAGERESS

Down letters: ANNUAL, POET, CAPUA, PEER, LITRS, AMERICANS column letters, ISAAC, ERIE, LOO, WAFERS, EMDS, SMS, GREEN, OKJM, ALD, QUI, etc.

## Detectives

1. James Hadley Chase, *No Orchids for Miss Blandish*, 1939
2. E. C. Bentley, *Trent's Last Case*, 1913
3. Sapper (H. C. McNeile), *Bulldog Drummond*, 1920
4. Nicholas Blake, *A Question of Proof*, 1935. This was the pseudonym of C. Day-Lewis, and this book was the first of his crime novels.
5. Agatha Christie, *The Murder of Roger Ackroyd*, 1926
6. Raymond Chandler, *The Long Good-Bye*, 1953
7. Dorothy L. Sayers, *Gaudy Night*, 1935
8. Michael Innes, *Death at the President's Lodging*, 1936. This is the pseudonym of J. I. M. Stewart, and this was the first book under the Innes name.
9. Arthur Conan Doyle, *A Study in Scarlet*, 1887. These are the very first words recorded by Dr John Watson.
10. G. K. Chesterton, 'The Blue Cross' – the first story in *The Innocence of Father Brown*, the first of the books.

## Quick-Fire Quiz

### Names of Authors and Characters

1. Mrs Hudson. Not to be confused with Hudson and Mrs Bridges, who appeared in *Upstairs, Downstairs*.
2. Reginald. This, it is revealed very far on into the saga, is how he is known in the Junior Ganymede club.

3. Smike – most memorably performed in the RSC production.

4. C. Day-Lewis. And despite his formidable reputation as a poet, it is these detective novels that are the most sought after by collectors.

5. Carrie – mother of Lupin, and survivor of Cummings and Gowing.

6. The Fool's term of endearment for his royal master, *King Lear*.

7. The initials were retained in each case; hence: Acton – Ann, Currer – Charlotte, Ellis – Emily.

8. Winston Smith. We do not know if this is a conscious reference to Churchill.

9. Raskolnikov – and, in common with number 8, most memorably portrayed by the actor John Hurt.

10. Mrs Hester Thrale, patron and friend to Samuel Johnson, and author of the *Anecdotes*. Her second marriage was to an Italian musician named Piozzi.

11. Piggy – he of the cracked spectacles, and the conch.

12. Mrs Malaprop, most certifiably.

13. James Graham
14. William Schwenk (yes, Schwenk)
15. Cicely Veronica
16. William Butler
17. Antonia Susan (Margaret Drabble's sister, actually)
18. Montague Rhodes
19. Phyllis Dorothy
20. Pelham Grenville

## The Grand General Book Quiz

1. Although the hardbound volume was offered at only three-and-six, a tear-off competition slip was included at the rear, whereby any reader (that is to say, *purchaser*) could win £500 by supplying the best explanation for the protagonist's death. The ploy worked, and 38,000 copies of the book were sold. Rather sad to have to add, then, that Wallace's confidence in the book had led him to spending hugely on promotion, this resulting in an overall loss of £1,400. A chastened Wallace then sold the book rights outright to Newnes for just £72, and Newnes – wouldn't you just know it – went on to sell hundreds of thousands of the things over the years, after Wallace had achieved fame and finally fortune from his subsequent books. He became hugely prolific, this leading P. G. Wodehouse to remark that nine hundred out of every thousand Wallaces were well worth the seven-and-sixpence charged.

2. Samuel Johnson writing on Pope's edition of Shakespeare of 1721. These lines, however, were written sixty years after in Johnson's *Lives of the Poets*, and did not at all represent the current viewpoint; indeed, it led to fresh accusations of Johnson having failed to keep abreast of Shakespeare scholarship. Johnson's own edition of the Bard had appeared in 1765, and in the course of the Preface he offers the following: 'The great contention of criticism is to find fault with the moderns, and the beauties of the ancients. While an authour is yet living we estimate his powers by his worst performance, and when he is dead we rate them by his best.' All of which might convince

us that the Doctor was a temperate, kind, gentle and unbigoted individual – epithets he would never have tolerated to his face.

3. Rupert Hart-Davis, during the course of his epic and highly entertaining correspondence with George Lyttelton, now published by John Murray in six volumes. The reply to this disservice to Ian Fleming ran as follows: 'I shall not read Ian Fleming's latest. He has really gone off the rails in the matter of murders and beatings, and tortures, and impossibility, and lust; Bond was becoming a bore in the last book, and must have made it by now.'

4. Suicide, fairly evidently. The first is extracted from Virginia Woolf's own suicide letter to her husband Leonard in 1941, while the second is a rather typical squib from Voltaire in an undated letter to Madame du Deffaud. Only the third occurs in fiction – one of the most painful episodes in a great, but agonizing novel – Thomas Hardy's *Jude the Obscure*. The eldest of Jude's three children has hanged the two younger, and then himself. The note is his.

5. This is the traditional date for the birth of William Shakespeare, in 1564, and also for the day he died, in 1616.

6. Humorists all, as you might have guessed. From the top, P. G. Wodehouse in his autobiographical book *Performing Flea* (1953), James Thurber, writing in the *New York Post* in 1955, Jerome K. Jerome in his memoirs *My Life and Times* (1927), Mark Twain – one of his many contributions to A. K. Adams's *The Home Book of Humorous Quotations* – and,

perhaps unexpectedly, Richard Brinsley
Sheridan, in a letter to David Garrick, of
1778.

7. A bit of a tricksy question, this one. *The Works
   of Max Beerbohm* was a small volume of
   essays, and was his very first published work,
   in 1896. As Max himself has observed: 'There
   is always something rather absurd about the
   past.'

8. Both from George Bernard Shaw. The sober
   castigation comes at the outset of his Preface
   to *Pygmalion* (1912) and the extraordinary
   phonetic howl comes from the mouth of none
   other than Eliza Doolittle in Act I of the ply.
   Sorry – *play*.

9. St Luke 12:19. But the 'for tomorrow we die'
   bit is wrongly attributed – although Isaiah
   did write, 'let us eat and drink, for tomorrow
   we die.' Either he thought that the merriment
   would take care of itself, or else that the eve of
   one's metaphorical demise was no time for
   horsing around.

10. It's old Ian Fleming again, writing in a style
    that was mercifully uncharacteristic (his de-
    tractors would say *bad*) in *The Spy Who Loved
    Me* (1962), billed as being written by Ian
    Fleming 'with Vivienne Michel'. The novel
    may barely be described as a James Bond book
    at all, as he only makes his appearance on
    page 137, and then with the hoot-making line:
    'I'm sorry. I've got a puncture.'

11. The sequence is named after the painting by
    Nicholas Poussin (1593–1665) now housed in
    the Wallace Collection. The idea is that time

is symbolized by the severely classical nature of the work(s), the dance being enjoined by the flow and the rhythm.

12. a. ... *Robinson Crusoe*, Daniel Defoe, 1719
    b. ... *Dr Jekyll and Mr Hyde*, R. L. Stevenson, 1886
    c. ... *Tom Jones* ..., Henry Fielding, 1749
    d. *Tess of the D'Urbervilles* ..., Thomas Hardy, 1891
    e. ... *Humphry Clinker*, Tobias Smollett, 1771
    f. ... *Moll Flanders*, Daniel Defoe, 1722
    g. ... *Tristram Shandy*, Laurence Sterne, 1759–67
    h. *Brideshead Revisited* ..., Evelyn Waugh, 1945
    i. *Twelfth Night* ..., Shakespeare, 1601(?), First Folio, 1623

13. W. H. Auden. Isn't it a peach?

14. A word used (but not invented) by Shakespeare in *Love's Labour's Lost*. Fairly understandably, it has become a spearhead of the 'Baconian Theory' – that held by those who believe that the plays of William Shakespeare were written by Francis Bacon. They see it as a cryptogram, the Latin rendering of which translates as 'These Plays, F. Bacon's Offspring, are Preserved for the World'. Tenuous at least, I should have thought, but particularly so when we learn from the Shakespearian scholar S. Schoenbaum that the word had anyway been used far earlier – as early as 1460, over seventy years before the birth of either Bacon or Shakespeare.

15. *a.* *The Ripening Seed*, Colette, 1923 (English edn 1949)
    *b.* *The Outsider*, Albert Camus, 1942 (English edn 1946)
    *c.* *In Camera*, Jean-Paul Sartre, 1945 (English edn 1946, reissued in 1946 under the title *No Exit*)
    *d.* *Strait is the Gate*, André Gide, 1909 (English edn 1924)
    *e.* *The Tin Drum*, Günter Grass, 1959 (English edn 1963)

16. *a.* Arthur Quiller-Couch
    *b.* Helen Gardner
    *c.* W. H. Auden
    *d.* Kingsley Amis
    *e.* W. B. Yeats
    *f.* Philip Larkin
    *g.* D. J. Enright
    *h.* Iona and Peter Opie
    *i.* Geoffrey Grigson
    *j.* Jon Stallworthy

17. They are both gentlemen's gentlemen. (I am, of course, thinking of Lord Peter Wimsey's manservant, and not the fat owl of the Remove.)

    As to the other daft little question – they are both Belgian.

18. *a.* Tennessee Williams, 1954
    *b.* Christopher Isherwood, 1945
    *c.* Tom Sharpe, 1974
    *d.* Malcolm Lowry, 1933
    *e.* W. H. Hudson, 1904
    *f.* William Thackeray, 1837–8
    *g.* Anthony Burgess, 1962
    *h.* Walter Scott, 1824
    *i.* Arthur Conan Doyle, 1887
    *j.* J. G. Ballard, 1971
    *k.* Thomas Pynchon, 1973

**19.** These are anagrams of young-blood authors. Armed with this knowledge, you may wish to go back and have another crack. But for the brilliant (who have already solved them) and for the idle (who deem life too short), here they are:

    *a.* A. N. Wilson
    *b.* Ian McEwan
    *c.* Salman Rushdie
    *d.* Martin Amis
    *e.* Anita Brookner

**20.** All suicides. Chatterton's is perhaps the most tragic of all, for having produced the 'Rowley' poems (verse purported to have been written by a medieval monk) he poisoned himself with arsenic in 1770 at the age of eighteen, apparently in despair over his poverty. Virginia Woolf walked into the Ouse at Sussex, never to return, in 1941. Sylvia Plath killed herself in London in 1963, a month after her only novel, *The Bell Jar*, was published, under the pseudonym of Victoria Lucas. Koestler and his wife committed suicide at home in London in 1983; they were members of EXIT, and supporters of euthanasia. John Berryman ended his life in Minneapolis, in 1972.

**21.**   *a.* – 6 Penelope Fitzgerald, *The Bookshop*
    *b.* – 10 C. P. Snow, *The Affair*
    *c.* – 1 Beryl Bainbridge, *The Dressmaker*
    *d.* – 7 L. P. Hartley, *The Boat*
    *e.* – 9 Philip Roth, *The Breast*
    *f.* – 4 Agatha Christie, *The Hollow*
    *g.* – 2 Brendan Behan, *The Scarperer*
    *h.* – 3 Saul Bellow, *The Victim*
    *i.* – 8 Iris Murdoch, *The Unicorn*
    *j.* – 5 Margaret Drabble, *The Millstone*

22. *a.* – 2 John Berryman, *Love and Fame*
    *b.* – 10 Siegfried Sassoon, *Sequences*
    *c.* – 5 Thom Gunn, *Fighting Terms*
    *d.* – 7 Robert Lowell, *Near the Ocean*
    *e.* – 1 W. H. Auden, *The Age of Anxiety*
    *f.* – 9 Ezra Pound, *Thrones*
    *g.* – 3 John Betjeman, *High and Low*
    *h.* – 6 Seamus Henney, *Wintering Out*
    *i.* – 4 Lawrence Durrell, *On Seeming to Presume*
    *j.* – 8 Louis MacNeice, *Holes in the Sky*

23. Not so straightforward, actually:
    *a.* *Joseph* Rudyard Kipling
    *b.* *Adeline* Virginia Woolf
    *c.* *Henry* Max(imilian) Beerbohm
    *d.* *Enoch* Arnold Bennett
    *e.* *Patrick* Branwell Brontë
    *f.* *Arthur Annesley* Ronald Firbank
    *g.* *Harry* Sinclair Lewis
    *h.* *Clarence* Malcolm Lowry
    *i.* *Helen* Beatrix Potter
    *j.* *Giles* Lytton Strachey
    *k.* *Richard Horatio* Edgar Wallace
    *l.* *Sidonie Gabrielle* Colette

24. *a.* George Meredith, 1891
    *b.* Lynne Reid Banks, 1974
    *c.* Bertolt Brecht, 1958
    *d.* T. S. Eliot, 1943
    *e.* Dorothy L. Sayers, 1931
    *f.* Luigi Pirandello, 1921
    *g.* William Empson, 1930
    *h.* Alistair Maclean, 1966
    *i.* Dorothy L. Sayers, 1934
    *j.* Agatha Christie, 1939